# Hell's Reaper

Hell's Reaper: Book One

ISBN: 9798816538350

Copy editing by Raven Quill Editing, LLC

Proofread by Cruel Ink Editing & Design

Re-edited and Proofread by LiSara Cool Editing

Cover Designed by Open World Cover Designs

Chapter header – Canva

Rune Hunt

# Hell's Reaper

# Asura

I hear the Zippo lighter flicker three times before finally sparking through the strange silence of the club. I try my best not to stiffen on stage. Usually, something like that would never catch my attention because I'm not a stranger to smoking in the club or during a performance, but that's another sign that *he's* here.

I'll be shocked if it's not him. At this point, two years later, I doubt he's changed much. He smells the same as if someone lit a campfire right next to his bed and the burning wood clung to his skin all day. His dark, heavy magic makes my spine stiffen. The only change is that I don't smell the cigarettes he usually smokes.

## Hell's Reaper

The lights dim to a red hue as the music begins to play.

*Of course, he had to come tonight out of all nights...*

I round the pole, feeling it move with each step. It's cold under my touch, as if someone else wasn't just on it. Stopping in front of it, I raise my arms over my head, press my back against it, and roll my body against the steel, ignoring the coldness on my spine.

He will *not* stand in the way of me and my money, and I know for sure he won't strike. *Not in front of all these humans.*

If he's anything like he was two years ago, he'd be uncomfortable with I'm flaunting my body. Being sexy is a job requirement, and I've perfected it down to a science. At first, this was a way for me to get money quickly, but now, it has allowed me to let loose and express myself. I've gotten much better at moving my hips, bouncing my ass, and even doing tricks on the pole.

I use my left arm to hold myself up as I spin my body around the side of the pole, letting it part my legs. Once my heels hit the ground, my hips dip, and I swing them to the beat. Using my upper body, I spin around, locking one of my knees around the pole as the other follows suit higher up. I let go with my upper body, reaching up and fluffing my hair while I spin around the bar using my knees. After a few rotations, I rewrap my legs, so the pole is between my core. And flip upside down into a bridge before standing to my feet.

I step away from the pole before dropping to my knees and crawling to the edge of the stage. Barely able to see the crowd with the spotlights on me. Sometimes it's good I don't notice who is in the crowd, but I want to know who's watching today.

I slide off the stage, loving the roar of the people. Swaying my hips on my way to the first guy who holds out a fifty, I dance on him briefly, showing him a bit of what he can get later.

*If I survive this.*

Then I move on.

A random hand in the aisle sticks out a hundred-dollar bill, catching my attention. As I move closer to him, his magic sends goosebumps over my exposed skin. *I know what he is.*

I lean down when I get in front of him, locking eyes as he slips the bill into the strap of my white bra. Afterward, I drop to my knees to the song's beat, using my palm to spread his legs apart.

A smirk curls upon his soft, pink lips.

As I reach his eye level again, I snake my body through his legs. "Shouldn't you stay hidden?" I whisper, knowing he can hear me over the drowning music because of *what* he is.

He cocks a brow, crimson eyes on me. "Why? You knew we were here the moment you came out on stage."

*He's right.*

Pushing his legs closed, I climb into his lap, thighs straddling each side of his. His warmth comforts me like a hug. When I roll my hips deeply, he sharply inhales near my ear. His cock grows between us, yet he doesn't seem to think twice about it. "We? Are you *actually* with him, *dog*?" I mutter into his ear, pressing my body flush against him.

He chuckles deeply, his chest rumbling against mine.

As I sway to the music, I twist my body, dropping my ass right against his bulge. I reach back; my fingertips feel the shaved sides of his head before fisting the top of his brown curls.

He lets out a huff of breath right against my ear, one of his hands grabbing my waist.

*Did I forget to say this guy is big? Mind out of the gutter… He's taller than me, and he's fucking sitting.*

"Are you trying to piss him off with this dance?" He chuckles into the shell of my ear.

I glance around the room, seeing the frown on his reaper's lips. "It's working."

When I get out of his lap, my body misses his warmth, and I instantly dive back for more. My fisted hand pulls his head back to look up at me. His shining red eyes squint as his full lips curl into a smirk. My eyes roam over his sharp square jaw, Adam's apple, wide, broad shoulders, and lower. His huge hands touch my bare thighs, and I feel his heat dance across

8

my skin. My eyes stop at the massive shaft poking me this whole time.

*Oh yeah. I wouldn't mind riding that pole...*

Pushing away from him, I sway back to the stage as the music dies. I smirk; my eyes meet the icy glare of the reaper. His dark eyes burn into me as his square jaw tightens.

*Oh, he's mad.*

In the back of the club, I quickly grab my stuff from my locker and then switch into my friend's shoes, sweats, and hoodie.

*They will throw them off my scent. That hound was only getting close to me to catch my scent, and I fell for it.*

I throw my bag of money over my shoulder before bolting for the back door.

"Alexa!" someone calls after me.

I ignore it. It's not even my real name, but close. I must return to my hotel and grab my stuff before leaving. Quickly, I push through the back door and run into a large *wall*. I blink, looking up, up, and *up* until I see the face of a new guy. He is definitely not as sexy as the one I danced on, but his magic tells me he's one of the guys after me.

"Damn... you're big," I mutter.

A smirk runs across his lips as he grabs my forearm and pulls me to the end of the alleyway.

"Hands off! *Hey*! Watch it!" I shout, drawing the attention of the bouncer. It's not the first time I've been grabbed outside the club.

"Hey, let her go!" One of them steps forward to my aid. I've always been grateful for them. They step in for the dancers a lot.

The guy removes his hands, and I take my chance to lift my knee fast and hit his thigh. Keeling over, he shouts as I reel back, punching him hard in the jaw and sending him to the ground.

I take the chance to rush out into the busy street. Once across the street, I dash toward my motel, clenching my money bag. It seems like the group had split up to cover all the exits, meaning they might not notice what I did to that guy or, depending on their bond, they felt it too.

*I know I won't get far, but I'm sure as hell going to put up a fight.*

Once at the crappy motel, I rush inside my room to grab the duffle bag that is always packed and ready and empty all my earnings from tonight into it. I'm used to constantly moving around and never staying in one place and being on the run for so long does get tiring. Initially, I would join groups of friends going out for drinks and dancing, but I quickly learned that my presence put humans at risk.

*Her blood sprayed against the red brick building.*

My blood runs cold, causing me to close my eyes and take a deep breath.

Since that night, I've learned to distance myself from everyone and everything.

I grab the keys to the room before moving back to the front door, but as soon as I open it, *he* is standing there with his dark eyes looking down at me.

Jolting, I slam the door shut or *try* to, and he pushes it open easily. Then his three *little* guards enter, filling me with nerves. *Little* isn't the word to describe these seven-foot-tall men.

"Hey. Looking taller, Khazon," I say nervously to the ringleader, but he doesn't speak. It has only been two years, but his appearance has changed significantly. His jaw is also much more defined, like his shoulders and muscles, bulging through his shirt and leather jacket. His dark brown hair is cut short, hanging against his face a bit. Not only is he taller, but he's also wider now. His dark—almost black—eyes blazing with hatred. "You know… four guys and one girl are not a good look if I scream right now."

"Do it," Khazon challenges, his voice way deeper than I remember.

"Oh, hey, you finally hit puberty!" I tease.

He rolls his eyes. "Just come with us, and you won't get hurt."

"Aren't you a sadomasochistic, though? Isn't that what all the Soul Reapers are?"

"No," he deadpans.

"*Sad.*" Dropping my duffle bag, I kick out at his jaw.

He grabs my foot before it can hit him. "Asura, stop these games."

11

"Games?" Rolling my shoulders as I pull back, I prepare myself for my next attack. I feel my bones crack before punching out but ceasing my movement and punching with my other hand. He dodges my sneak attack. "These aren't games, Khazon."

I try to catch him off guard with another attack, but Khazon grabs my fist, pulling me hard into his chest. "Yes, they are! You're acting like a child, not the heir."

Wiggling my hands-free from his grasp, I lift my knee and hit his side. He doesn't wince. "Fucking hell, do I have to hit you in the nuts?"

He pushes me away, rolling his eyes. "We aren't kids anymore. I've been training for the last two years to be better than you and to bring you back."

"Kinky," I deadpan. "I couldn't care less, Khazzie. Take your massive dogs and get out!"

The one from the bar raises a brow, smirking. I bite my bottom lip to keep from smiling. *Was he smiling at the word I used, massive? I meant it in both ways.*

"Come easy, and I won't be forced to take you down," Khazon says, drawing my attention back to him. I tend to get sidetracked a lot.

I smirk, raising my fists and using my elbows to cover my ribs. *I've trained too—sort of...* I throw a punch, aiming for his chest. "Don't get a boner doing it, Khazzie."

He grabs it, twisting my wrist behind my back before pushing me into the dresser. My hips feel a slight sting at the pressure. Jaw tightening, I stomp down on his right foot, then launch my head back into his jaw. He groans, stumbling back toward the bed. "Asura!"

I cock a brow. *I know for a fact I can't get past six-foot-two Khazon and his three seven-foot bodyguards, but I won't go down without a fight.*

"Don't touch her," Khazon orders one of his goons.

I glance over, seeing the one I hit in the street reaching out for me. "Oh, be a dear. Return this key." I throw the room key. He catches it but stares at me. "Oh, fuck, sorry. You can't think for you—"

Khazon charges into me, lifting me over his shoulder. I wrap my leg around his chest and hit him hard in the neck with my fist. He slams me onto the dresser, throwing a fist at me. I lift my leg, quickly wrapping it around his arm and holding it down. His other fist flies, and I dodge it just in time for him to shatter the mirror behind me.

I wince as the glass falls against my back, and that's when I realize how much stronger he actually is and how much he wants to hurt me right now. "Damn…"

He looks up at me, his dark eyes blazing with rage.

"If you wanted me to come with you so badly, you could have just asked," I tease.

He stares at me. "You've hurt too many men for me to take you lightly."

13

The smirk slides from my lips. I was defending myself, but I'd rather not tell him and his goons that story. Save that for a rainy day. "It's what I do, and I'll leave on a few conditions."

"No." He pulls back, straightening his jacket.

I glance down at his knuckles to see how severely he's hurt, but he's not. He heals so quickly now. Overall, he's gotten faster, smarter, and better than I am now. He's a reaper; He has to be. "Then I won't go."

He cocks a brow. "You think you can *really* overpower all of us?"

"I *know* I can; I have a taser and mace, Khazzie. Now… One, I want that key returned, so they don't take any more of my money because now I have to pay to fix this mirror."

Khazon rolls his eyes but looks at the guy that has the key. He huffs, leaving the room to go to the front desk.

"Two, you take me to the waffle diner here on Earth."

He cocks a brow.

"It could be one big date or whatever, but I'm hungry, and I'm not going to Hell on an empty stomach. Transporting always makes me feel sick."

Khazon pinches the bridge of his nose, sighing. "Asura… You have thirty minutes at that stupid waffle house."

I gasp, touching my chest. "Not stupid! And I won't even need that long. I come quickly when syrup is involved."

He steps back, letting me jump from the dresser. Glass clatters to the ground. "After you, Princess of Hell."

A moan escapes my lips while eating the best
cinnamon roll waffles I've ever had. The old-fashioned
waffle house is empty at this late hour, allowing the
three large guards to sit at the counter away from us.
Khazon sits in front of me at one of the uncomfortable
red booths, rubbing his headache away with two
fingers.

"Do you want some?" I offer stabbing a piece
on my fork before holding it out for him.

He looks up at me, dark eyes burning into me.
"No."

I roll my eyes, eating it myself. "Come on,
Khazzie, and I'm buying."

"Because you're made of money now? Why do you even do... *that*?" he says, sounding very grumpy that I had been stripping. *Cute.*

I set down my fork, licking my lips as I lean in. "I made a few hundred dollars on Saturday and Sunday last week. Do you know how many men would kill to see me dance? I've gotten better over the last two years, and I can tell what a guy wants by just looking at them." My eyes scan up and down his body, and I can tell what he needs–A dominant woman.

"It's kind of *degrading*, don't you think?"

I snort. "No. Men will look at me either way, and you might as well make them pay. And it raised my confidence in my body and sexuality tenfold. I don't feel degraded, and I feel empowered." My voice catches the guards' attention—the hell hounds. That's who guards the Soul Reapers—three hellhounds of their choosing. They feel what each other feels and heal with each other's magic. They don't even need to speak for one of them to know what the reaper is thinking. It's a sacred bond that I will never understand.

I pull out my phone, pulling up that app for the club where people can send you tips online. "I made almost four hundred dollars from one dance tonight. Imagine if I was able to do my whole set for the night." Most nights are never this good, and some nights I leave with less money than I had. But then there are some nights, like tonight, where everyone in town is there, and the night is going smoothly until four supernatural beings crash the fun.

Although I am raving about the money, the club life sucks. Between the bruises from the poles and the hells to the incessant sexual assault we deal with, the money doesn't amount to much—and it certainly doesn't make up for the downfalls of the club life. But at the end of the day, hard work pays off. I'm paid, and my confidence is higher. Something about dancing and letting go on or off the pole makes me feel free.

He glances at the phone, rolling his eyes. "Don't care."

I roll my eyes and go back to eating.

One of his hellhounds turns to talk to us, the cute one from the club. "So, you guys know each other?"

I nod, just as Khazon says, "No."

My brow cocks. "Khazon and I grew up together. We were inseparable."

"Until you left," he deadpans.

A sliver of guilt runs through me, but I shove more waffles into my mouth to push it down. "Shit happens, but it seems like *someone* is still hurt by it." I turned to the guy. "Did Khazon pick you or…? And what are your names, dogs?"

"Ledger," the cute one from the club says, smiling at me. "Master picked us himself."

"Master? I knew he was a freak," I tease, but I can tell Ledger called him that as a joke.

"The other two are Eames and Andrew," he says. But he can probably tell that I'm not interested in them. They aren't as pretty as Ledger; he looks almost unreal. Tall and broad, more than Khazon is now. He leans against the counter, sipping his coffee as his red eyes run over me. Jet black curls fall against his ivory forehead.

*Oh, the things I would do to him... I'd make him my bitch for the night and torture him with a harsh edging until he's begging and—*

"Stop looking at my hound like he's your last waffle." Khazon snaps at me.

Slowly, I pry my eyes from his guard and look up at him. "I see being an anima *whatever* has their perks. Maybe I'll become one to have hot hellhounds I can fuck too."

"Anima *Messorms*," Khazon corrects, fixing his uniform. I glance down, seeing all the tactical gear hidden under the standard leather jacket. I faintly see the symbol of the academy on his chest—the grim reaper skull with a vine circling it, "and I don't *fuck* my hounds. They are here to help and protect me, not for sex."

I was the ripe age of eighteen when I left home. It was the age I could have gone to Grim Reaper's Soul Reaper Academy to become a reaper, and I refused, knowing if I did, I'd be closer to being the heir, and I didn't want that.

"Sad," I say with a smile and glance at Ledger, who smiles back. My eyes go back to Khazon, who is glaring at me. "So, you're at least a level one anima *whatever* because they'd never let you out otherwise."

"Level two."

My brows bounce. "That quickly?"

"I was motivated," Khazon says, eyes hard on me.

I snort. "You wanted the satisfaction of finding the heir so that you can get brownie points with Daddy?"

He smirks, leaning in. "And I knew you'd never hurt me like the others."

I don't let his comment get to me. I've hurt a lot of Soul Reapers—Anima Messorms—in the past. I didn't mean to, for a few of them, and I was actually defending myself from one.

Khazon has Ledger, and the other two I forgot the names of. Usually, it's a mutual agreement between the reaper and hellhounds; however, there have been occasions where the hounds were forced into service.

"I could have hurt you," I finally say, but it comes out more like a whisper.

"You could have... And we both know in your natural form, you're stronger."

I shrug.

"So, why did you let us take you?" Ledger butts in.

I lean back, throwing my hands behind my head. "I plan on trying to escape at least a few times."

Khazon growls at that, almost sounding like a hellhound. His jaw is taunted, and his eyes are blazing with rage hotter than Hell's flame. Having Khazon mad at me so much is a complete one-eighty of what he was like before. He was always so gentle and kind, but something changed him.

"But I missed you and knew you liked waffles, so…"

We lock gazes, and I wait for his to soften, but it never does. "Finish eating, Asura," he orders.

Just as I am about to go back to eating, the door opens with a ding. My eyes look up as the air stiffens with dark magic.

*We are dark…but they are darker.*

Draco's lifeless black eyes land on me, and he smirks, sharp fangs flashing. Ice dumps into my veins as my heart begins to skip a beat. He winks and sits at a booth, obviously hearing the pounding in my chest.

*Blood sprays against the brick wall as her screams become gargled. His teeth are embedded into her skin as his lifeless eyes stare at me.*

Khazon doesn't even have to look over his shoulder to know *what* is here. "Pay, and let's go."

I nod, pulling out a fifty from my bra strap and putting it on the table. Quickly, I swallow my last bite and stand.

Draco stands simultaneously, earning a growl from one of Khazon's hounds. I haven't seen these men—the Blood Clan—in too long. They rarely come out, only at night, or their skin will burn–typical vampires without all the glittery skin. Supernatural beings have always been a thing from the beginning, and some have even learned to fit in with humans. The Blood Clan is the exception. They never fit in. Not in Hell, not on Earth. Honestly, Draco looks like he stepped out of Hot Topic after his parents gave him money and said, "Spend it wisely." *Spoiler: he did not.*

"Oh, hey! The Princess of Hell, Angel of Death, and his little hellhounds," Draco says a little too *fucking* loudly, allowing the diner workers to hear. Luckily, they probably think he's on something, and they are too busy cleaning up in the kitchen to notice us. When the vampire steps forward, so does Khazon, squeezing between us.

I can protect myself, but I let him do what he wants. If he wants to step between a vampire and me, go ahead.

"Just leave us alone, Draco," Khazon orders with authority I've never seen before. Khazon was a very small and timid child. He feared everything and anything, and as we got older, he got better at masking it, but I could always tell when he was scared.

"Once I get your girl," Draco says, pointing to me. "I'm officially a royal Blood. I've been looking for you, Princess." He flashes his fangs, and his friends behind him follow suit.

Magic swirls in the air. "How about we take this outside where there aren't humans?" Khazon's deep voice rumbles.

Rune Hunt

I glance at his shoulders, waiting for wings to come out. *Is this his magic? Has he really changed this much in the last two years?*

Draco snaps his fingers, and his two goons behind him disappear and reappear a moment later, blood dripping down their chins. In the kitchen, off to our left, three *thuds* come.

Ledger growls deeply as the smell of death fills the air. *They killed the humans.*

I stiffen, stepping back into Ledger's chest. The smell of something burning reaches my nose and makes me look at the portable heater hellhound behind me. Ledger's rage has him basically burning through his clothing.

"Now, give us the girl," Draco snarls.

Magic surges, catching my attention. Horns sprout from Khazon's dark hair, spiraling outwards to the back of his head. His skin grows an eerie black, but only around his hands, neck, and chin. He's not entirely shifted. Khazon reaches out, and something appears from thin air. Out comes a blazing red battle ax with two half-circle blades coming from the handle.

"A telum..." I gasp, eyes widening. I remember Khazon and me being kids, gushing about who would have the better telum—a weapon all Soul Reapers can conjure up—and now, he technically does. One of Draco's goons attacks first, rushing at Khazon. One of Khazon's hounds runs forward just as fast, wrapping his hand around the guy's neck and twisting harshly.

23

The guy thuds onto the ground, dead. Well, more dead than he was.

I step back more, blinking. The other vampire behind Draco disappears, and I bump into something solid behind me. I glance at the others who, aside from the vampire, are all in front of me. My stomach drops, and the hairs on the back of my neck stand.

*Fuck... he's behind me, isn't he?*

Like a horror movie, I twist around, seeing the vampire behind me. He grasps my throat, pulling me into the air. I gasp sharply before lifting my leg and kicking him in the jaw. He blinks at me, barely phased.

Khazon acts fast by slicing the vampire's arm clean off with his crimson ax.

Scrambling backward, I bump into Ledger's back as he growls at Draco.

My stomach rumbles with lust, earning a quick glare from Ledger. *I can't help it that men who growl are hot.*

"Better give up now, Draco," Khazon says. "Before you die tonight."

I glance at Draco, who weighs his options, but a smirk lets me know that he's made his choice and he isn't going to go down easily.

Draco attacks.

Ledger shifts into hellhound form; his bones crack as his limbs elongates, clothing shedding from his body. Quicker than I can think, a hellhound with glowing red eyes sits in front of me. Even on all fours, his body is almost touching my face. He has little to no

24

fur along his ash-brown body and long pointed ears. Sharp bone spikes travel down his spine all the way to his tail. He attacks, snapping harshly on Draco's arm, the vampire claws at his face, blood spraying.

Khazon grunts behind me, drawing my attention; one of his other hounds has shifted and is by his side, fighting a vampire.

I feel useless as the last hound is by my side, protectively but ready to jump in whenever needed.

I can take down these vampires; I've had to before. The vampires have hurt me one too many times, and I've finally figured out how to mask my scent from them. This time, they probably followed Khazon and his hounds.

*Thud!*

Ledger's hellhound body hits the counter. He looks worse than I thought he would. Blood drenches his body, and only one of his eyes opens, the other swollen shut.

"Use it, Ledge!" Khazon shouts.

His open red eye flickers to his leader before he stands and lets out a roar. The injuries don't seem to faze him as his skin becomes ablaze with a blood-orange fire. A gasp catches in my throat as I feel the heat of his magic. He roars again, fire spitting from his ignited mouth.

The hellhound next to me nudges me to the exit at the front, and between the two hounds and fire, Draco can't get to me. The cold slaps me in the face as we both step outside. Khazon and the other hounds follow, with Ledger at the head, spitting fireballs against the floor. The diner goes up in flames with the vampires—who look desperate to escape—still inside.

Twisting to move the car, I hit something solid and cold. Gasping, I step back. *More?*

He stares down at me, crimson eyes wandering over my face. Like the hellhounds, he's tall, but maybe not as tall. His long, pure white hair is pulled back into a low ponytail. Lips curling around his unlit cigarette, he cocks a brow. "Asura."

"Thorne," I reply almost breathlessly. It's been a while since I've seen him. Since Draco killed my only human friend, Thorne seems always to be around to keep his brother, Draco, out of trouble… as if that helps.

Khazon pushes me back and steps between us. "Back off, Thorne."

Cigarette in mouth, he raises his hands and steps back.

Khazon pushes me to the car. "Get in," he orders.

I want to mock him, but my eyes stay glued to Thorne. The vampire watches me with a slight smirk curling on his lips.

"See you, Asura," he mutters. Slowly, he pries his eyes from me and begins moving toward his brother. He raises a hand and flips open a familiar–looking Zippo lighter.

I slide into the back seat as the hellhounds pile in after me. Khazon gets behind the wheel, starting the

SUV and peeling out of here before we can even speak.

Jerking with the reckless driving, I hiss when Ledger's arm bumps mine. He's hotter than he usually is. "Sorry," he mutters, rolling down the window for the cool air. He had shifted back into his human form after encountering Thorne, and now his skin smokes against the cold air.

"Hell's fire hound?" I look at him before noticing he's butt naked next to me. His body is built to protect someone. His shoulders are broad and look grabbable. My stomach heats up when I think about digging my nails into them. His body is riddled with muscles, with abs lining his stomach to his deep hip indents. Running my eyes lower, I take in his dick size. His dick is very long, even though it's not hard.

"Hey! Stop it!" Khazon orders, hitting me in the head with extra clothing.

I glance up at Ledger, handing over the clothes. "Oops. My bad."

He smirks, not seeming to care.

I keep my eyes averted, letting them all get dressed. I lean forward toward Khazon. "How come you didn't fully shift to get your telum? Isn't that only something demonic beings can touch?"

Khazon let out a sigh. "I can't control the Angel of Death yet."

I blink at him. *That makes two of us now.*

Slowly, his hands pat his jacket.

"*Motherfucking* vampire took my Zippo lighter."

27

## Hell's Reaper
A smirk creeps across my face.

## Asura

*Hell, sweet Hell.*

Hell isn't how it is imagined. Yeah, things are on fire, and there're cliffs at every turn, but it's divided into a few different places, like the Palace of Hades in the east. It's nicer now that Persephone does the decorating. It's still all gothic and sad looking, but it's like gothic chic with flowers everywhere. She has miles and miles of fields full of fruit and flowers. I loved going there as a kid, hanging out with their son, and eating everything I could find until I got into trouble.

Then you've got Satan's Palace. Everything there is on fire, I swear. He lives deep in the mountains toward the north and rarely leaves his home. The river,

Styx, divides him and Hades because they tend not to get along.

Then there's Lucifer. Kind of the hottest if you ask me. None of the underworld Kings are related to me, thank God. The things I'd let Lucifer do to me are a sin. That's all I have to say about him. His palace is all red and black, the colors of a sex dungeon.

Then there's the Devil in the center. Dad likes to show off that he is stronger than all of them. Technically he rules the underworld while the others control their sections and jobs. My father is the true representation of Hell. The dark caverns that surround the house have spikes below them. His castle looks dark and tall, and there's a spike everywhere—not precisely safe for kids.

"Can we go visit Hades?" I ask Khazon as we trudge up the hill to my father's palace. One wrong step and you fall into the spikes before the lava eats away at your skin.

I'm used to it.

"No," he deadpans.

"But I want to see Cerberus!" I whine.

"You're not a kid anymore, Asura. Stop acting like it."

I nod. "So, how about Lucifer? I heard he might have a stripping pole in his throne room; how true do you think that is?"

Khazon lets out a huff.

"Very real," Ledger answers, looking down at me. He's clothed now, sadly. "His son goes to the academy and says so."

I gasp. "Aw! Little Aragon goes to the academy?"

"No, the other one."

I pause for a second. "Jude?"

He shakes his head.

"Theron?"

He nods. "But the other *other* one, too."

"Lucifer has been busy," I mutter. "Ezekiel?"

"Bingo!"

I gasp, touching my head as we walk up the dark stairs of the palace. "I bet he's so hot now."

"He looks like his father," Ledger says.

I fan myself. *Did it just get ten degrees hotter in here?* "Who else goes there?"

Khazon sighs. "Your siblings, the Grim Reaper's daughters, and Hades's son."

"Ozias?" I gasp. "You're lying! I need to go. That academy seems hotter than Hell!"

He growls. "They *actually* want to be there and take it very seriously. I doubt your father will let you go after the shit you've been pulling."

I roll my eyes, catching a glimpse of the Shadow Guards. They blend in with the rock towers that surround the palace. When hired, each one was given the power to blend in with their surroundings on top of their birth powers. The large doors begin to open with a heavy groan that spreads so far that all the dead souls would be able to hear it. They groan along with it. "You forgot to realize I'm Daddy's little girl. He'd never—"

"Asura!" The Gates of Hell open with my father's booming voice. I freeze and stiffen. Being my father's eldest child and only daughter, I never got yelled at in my life. I've created so much trouble, but not one time did he ever get mad.

Khazon pats my back. "Good luck."

"Uh... You're not coming in?"

"And deal with his wrath? Fuck, no," he says, but there is a smirk on his face as he leads the group down the front stairs.

My lips part as I look at his strong, wide back; he's changed a lot. He was small and scrawny as a child, and now he's big and broad. "It was nice... seeing you again, Khaz..."

He pauses but doesn't look back. I know he's hurt that I left because I never explained why or even said goodbye. As much as I joke with him, I miss him every day. We were best friends. "Whatever. Bye, Asura."

I roll my eyes, waiting for them to go back down the pathed hill to the Styx River. After a moment, I move inside the castle to my father's throne room.

The throne room is made of pure black obsidian, covering the floors, walls, and ceiling. Rainbows dance across the black floor because of the stained glass, and the flames burn brightly outside. My father sits on the highest and largest velvet throne at the head of the room, and my three brothers sit beside him with two on one side.

Stepping into the middle of the room, I lift my chin high. "Father..."

He stares at me in his pure demon form. His large horns extend farther than his head and body. His entire body is a deep red, almost nearing black; his black eyes stare at me. I can literally see steam coming out of his nose with every huff. He stands, gripping the armrest. "Asura... You left your duties, went off to Earth, became a... stripper... and—"

I wince at "stripper." Not something you want your father to know. But I am twenty now, so I was and am an adult.

He huffs a harsh breath before his shoulders sag. "And I missed you, my little diaboli!" He throws his arms up.

A smirk runs across my lips as I drop my bag and move to him.

He captures me in his large warm arms, enveloping me. "I missed you! Were you eating well? Did you drink enough water? You must have had it so hard!"

Derrick, the second eldest, scoffs. "You would think she's the baby with how much she gets away with."

"Oh, nonsense! Kids sometimes must find themselves before they become the Emperor of Hell. I did it!" my father says, setting me down.

Finally, I breathe out.

"I ran from your pop and *actually* met a lot of cute females." My father sits. "It's normal for heirs to get cold feet."

I swallow... *Yeah, cold feet.* "You can yell at me, Dad. I left without even saying goodbye."

Derrick stands, eyes narrowing on me. "And she injured multiple reapers! She created havoc, and she's getting away with it. Punish her!"

My father cocks a brow. "How?"

"Whip her. Ground her. Something! Be a father, not a friend."

"That's enough from you, Derrick. You're excused."

My brother's eyes narrow on me before he turns away. His dark hair plops against his forehead and sharp ears with each step. Derrick is half-demon and half-elf, and when his mother passed, he came to live with us. He's hated me since day one, and the feeling is mutual. It seems like he's definitely gotten worse than he was in the last two years. He huffs before he and the rest of the siblings leave.

Fenric, the youngest, catches a sneak peek at me before the door closes behind them. A smirk runs across my face.

"I should punish you. Do you know how worried you made me?" my father says sternly. He can change his emotions quickly.

I let out a sigh. "I just thought…"

Rune Hunt

He waits for me to continue, but I don't. He's always been so patient with me. That's what made him a good ruler. I could never be like him. He keeps Hell and the supernatural beings that live here in line. "Do you want to be the heir, Asura? You are set to claim the throne in the next few years or so."

*Or so?* With a sigh, I speak, "You'll always be the best ruler. You have solved so many wars and run Hell so well...I can never amount to the man you are."

He chuckles. "Well, you're not a man."

I smile but instantly hang my head.

My father sighs, standing and shifting into his human form before standing in front of me. His hair is slicked back, silver from age. His dark eyes run over me as he moves close. My father is a tall man, no matter what form he's in. Running along his ivory skin are the flames of Hell. They swirl into symbols, burning a bright auburn with power. "What did you see, my child?"

*Fuck, he knows.* I swallow, eyes watering. "I don't know what I saw..."

He stays silent, letting me know I can continue when I'm ready.

"Two years ago, I had a vision that Hell would fall under my reign when I became Queen. Hell... actually turns into *hell*. Fire everywhere, palaces collapsing, souls escaping Hell... It wasn't good." I whisper the last part. Since I turned sixteen, I have developed the ability to see the future; the next in line to reign always does.

35

My father nods. "Then you left because of it?"

I look up at him, tears threatening to fall. "If Hell is set to fall under my reign, why would I accept the throne?"

He circles me. "But you came back?"

"Hell… is set to fall under Derrick's reign too." I close my eyes, sighing. "Hell will fall no matter what, but I don't know how we can stop it."

My father nods. "We will have to tell the other courts of Hell, so they are aware."

I nod.

"I have a vision myself, diaboli," he says, pacing.

I cock a brow, waiting for him to continue.

"I had a vision of what you need to do next. You need a court of people who will protect you."

My eyes roll. "I don't need protection. I can—"

"You also need to learn how to protect yourself better."

Looking up at him, I try to figure out what he means. My father can't teach me how to fight like he did when I was a kid. Well, even then, he had trained people who taught us. "What was the vision, Father?"

"Hell is set to fall, no matter what, my child. I saw you with a team of men who would die to protect you."

I blink. I know no man who would even get a cut to protect me, let alone die. "I don't need men to protect me. I can figure out how to protect myself."

He sighs. "Anima Messorms Academy. You were wearing the uniform. Hellhounds protect you when you claim the throne, diaboli."

I look down. "You think I should go to Soul Reaper Academy?"

My father touches my chin and lifts my head. "Head up, or your crown will fall… I am giving you the okay to go to the academy to save Hell."

"How do you know it will save it?"

My father shrugs. "You won't know if you don't try."

I feel like my father is holding information from me, but I can't tell what, and I doubt he will tell me.

"Plus, you've always wanted to go… But tonight, we will feast as a family again." He smiles at me, tousling my hair.

For the next few minutes, I take my time looking at the changes inside the house; there isn't much. Then I go to my room. It is how it was when I left it, besides the small child crying on my bed. My younger brother, Fenric, sits up, eyes wet with tears. "Are you going to leave me again?"

I push out my bottom lip, rushing to him and wrapping my arms around him. I am a sucker for kids, especially him. We were inseparable when I was around. "I'll be starting school, but we will have visits often. Okay?"

Hell's Reaper

He burst into tears, hugging me. He was ten when I left, and now he's shy of thirteen. "We missed you."

I kiss his forehead. "I missed you too."

"You're going to the academy?" Derrick's voice comes from the open door of the room.

"Mhm," I hum, looking at him.

"Of course, he's letting you. You should be punished."

I almost growl. "I don't know what is with your sick twisted fantasy of me getting tortured, but it's not cool here."

"I'm sick and tired of you getting away with everything. The golden fucking child, my ass. You don't deserve that throne."

I twist around. "And you do?"

His brows pull together. "I would have had it if you didn't come back."

I cover Fenric's ears. "Get the fuck out of my room, Derrick."

He stares at me with disgust before he leaves. The fucker should be happy we took him in instead of letting him burn in the pits of Hell, but Dad is a softy for his kids. I let out a sigh, hoping tonight would be better.

The dinner feast is *actually* fun. My dad makes me sit next to him, and they go over things I missed out on. I love seeing them all smiling and in a good mood. My other brother, Killian, talks to me like I never left. We all had been close, minus Derrick. My father asks about my experiences on Earth, but I doubt a father wants to hear about a daughter's stripping experience. But I tell him about the waffle house I like, all the different places I've been to, and all the cool people I've met. Walking into my room, I lock the door behind me, not trusting Derrick as far as I can throw him. Fucker might try to kill me for my seat at the throne. My body aches to be inside the massive tub in the bathroom that looks like it could fit multiple people. I begin blasting the scorching water.

The large mirror next to the tub catches my reflection and my human form staring back at me. My skin is light bronze, and my long wavy hair is silver. I kind of look like my demon form, minus the deep purple skin, black curling horns, and long luscious tail. My lips are pink and full, while my button nose is small but wide. I have a few piercings in my nose, lips, and ears.

I pull off my dress, stripping down to my underwear. I've gained a lot of muscle from being a dancer. My pierced breasts shrank a few cup sizes, leaving me with a handful. My waist is small, though my hips are wide. I worked out a lot to be able to do so many tricks on the pole. My eyes glance at the various scars covering my body that will never fully heal from the countless fights with vampires or Soul Reapers. My fingers dance across my collarbone. Even humans from the club were rough with me.

*A voice in my head says, should have let me kill him when I had the chance.* I blink, knowing who it is.

## Hell's Reaper

I open the medicine cabinet, seeing my father stocked it with medicine I've been taking since I was a kid. I took every last pill when I left for Earth. Luckily, my father always had the cabinet stocked; I could have lasted a few more years before I ran out. I twist the pill bottle's lid and pop the tiny white pill in my mouth, swallowing it dry.     That will get rid of her for a while.

# Asura

My father, the devil, lays a sweet kiss on my cheek just as we pull up to the academy after a short teleporting drive that Monday morning. "I'm going to miss you, diaboli," my father says. He did the exact same thing and said the *exact same* thing to Fen. I think he might not have favorites anymore. "Oh! Killian, do you want kisses?" My father swoons. It is always so weird to have the devil as a father, and although he can be scary, he is a sucker for his kids.

"I'd rather die," Killian deadpans.

While my father is distracted, getting his heart broken, I slip from the car. My eyes wander to the academy in front of me.

## Hell's Reaper

*Soul Reaper Academy.* Sizeable black metal fences surround the whole campus, stretching as far as I can see. The main building sits smack dab in the middle of the campus, towering over everything else. The beige building has pillars that climb into a pointed peak, with windows covering each floor. Right in front is a large beige fountain with a statue of the Grim Reaper; He's full of himself sometimes.

My eyes move to the building beside it, showing off a scythe symbol in the front–Soul Reaper's dorms. The building looks the same, but less… pointy, and the drab color follows the colors of the gothic academy. Beside the dorms is a vast training field already filled with multiple groups.

My eyes land on a guy shifting into a hellhound. He shifts the same way Ledger did; his limbs extend until he's bent over on all fours. He shakes out the long coat of fur, eyes looking for his reaper.

I've dreamt of going to this place since I was a kid. Khazon, the son of Death, and Ozias, the son of Hades, would sit with me, talking about what powers our hellhounds would have. I never cared. I just wanted them. I wanted to be one of the best Soul Reapers like my father was. Before my father was the ruler of Hell, he went here. He leveled up quickly, collecting souls for the Shadow World to function.

"Oh, okay. Bye, kiddos. Dad loves you!" My father brings me back to reality. "Asura?"

Rune Hunt

I twist around to look at him. His bright blue eyes soften on me.

"Call me every day, and don't forget dinner every Saturday night."

I smile and nod. "Love you, Devil." I close the car door, and as soon as I'm away, his car disappears back to Hell with his surge of magic.

Derrick pushes past Killian and me, splitting us apart. I growl inhumanly at him, but he ignores us.

"Mess hall," Killian says, pointing to the building next to the academy as we walk in together, and I nod. "Someone will show you around more, but I can show you to the office."

Little to no people sit outside, but as soon as we walk through the doors, the halls are loaded with students. The students part like a sea as soon as their eyes land on me, filling the air with childish whispers. Lifting my chin, I continue after Killian.

I pass a group that parts just enough for me to see Khazon. His face darkens, and his jaw tightens, making him look so... handsome. I would never admit that two years ago, we were just best friends, nothing more. But two years have done him good. Now, it feels as if we're nothing more than strangers.

I wave my fingers sweetly, twisting to do so. *Where's his hot hellhound?* I turn to bump into something solid and warm—almost hot.

"So, you *really* did show?" Ledger's voice comes. *Here he is.*

Stepping back, I look up. "I just can't get enough of you."

He smirks. "Either that, or you love seeing Khazon mad."

My teeth pull in my bottom lip, feeling the vertical labret piercing. "A little bit of both."

He chuckles, licking his lips and looking down at me. The height difference between us is almost insane. I'm five-foot-five, and Ledger is at least seven-foot tall; Hellhounds are naturally that tall.

My eyes drop to his body. Today, he's wearing a short black sleeve button-up, showing off the veins running to his fingertips. Muscles bulge to break free from the sleeves. He has on khaki pants, and I bet if he turns around, his ass will look so good. Ledger seems like the type to work out his whole body, not just his arms. His short black hair is pushed back, showing off the jewelry lining his ears. "Where are you off to?"

"Office, I guess. My brother..." I peek around him to see Killian, but he's completely gone. My jaw drops. Honestly, a part of me forgot about him being here anyways. "Ass. He *was* taking me there."

Ledger smiles. "Just ask, and I'll take you. You don't have to lie."

I almost snorted, but I look up at him with innocent doe eyes. "Pretty please? I'm a very lost girl."

"Being seen with you is going to bring down my reputation with the ladies," he teases. "This will cost you."

44

When he turns, I glance down at his round ass before following him. *I'm a simple woman to please, that's for sure.* I flip my silver hair when I catch up. "Oh, no. How will I ever repay you?"

He smirks, glancing down at me. "I'll figure it out."

I nod, glancing at an even angrier Khazon. "Are you and Khazon *actually* friends?"

Ledger snorts, running his ringed fingers through his messy hair. "No. Khazon is friends with all the stuck-up, rich demons, and I'm just a lowly hellhound."

*A lowly hellhound?* "That breathes fire. You're basically a dragon."

He shakes his head. "He's just our Soul Reaper, and we don't really talk outside of him giving orders."

I sigh. "He's changed. I saw all those demons around him practically drooling. It's sad; he never cared about popularity."

Ledger shrugs, opening a door that leads to an office, motioning me through. "If he has people worshiping the ground he walks on, they won't leave him, as a certain *someone* did."

*Is it really my fault that Khazon changed as a person? No, Khazon is his own man.* I scoff. "Whatever."

"I'll see you around, *princess.*"

I hold the door, peeking around it to watch him walk away. My dark eyes travel from his wide, broad shoulders to his round ass. *The things I would do to him...*

He looks back as if he can hear my thoughts and flashes me a smile.

Giggling, I wink at him. The last thing I need to be is that feral demon that springs on every hot hellhound in sight. Because I *am* that feral demon, and I haven't had good sex in too fucking long.

I ignore my horny thoughts, moving to the front counter in the dean's office.

"Name?" the receptionist asks without looking up.

"Asura Beelzebub."

The receptionist looks up quickly with wide eyes. "Oh, uh. Hello, Princess." She averts her eyes.

I smile. "Hello. I'm supposed to have a room being set up for me."

She nods, looking down at her computer. "Mhm. It seems like you are sharing a room, though. I'm sure we can fit you in somewhere, but I might have to move some students to get you a room alone."

I shake my head. "Don't bother. I'll make friends. I don't mind sharing a room."

"A-Are you sure, miss?"

I nod. "Whatever you got. It's my fault for being so late."

She nods, doing some work on the computer. "SR 101 is your first class; once there, the professor will tell you what you need to do to advance. You might have to catch up on a few things. Uh...What's your clothing size?"

After telling her, she lets me use the bathroom to change. I feel like I'm in a cheesy porno with the red plaid skirt and the white button-up. At least it has the scythe logo over my left breast: two scythes in an x.

The receptionist is waiting for me with the paper with my classes on it. "I will have someone take your bag to the door, so you won't miss class."

"Thank you. What's your name?"

She swallows hard. "Uh, Miss Shay."

I nod. I see her pointed ears, alerting me she's fae. "Thank you, Miss Shay."

She smiles warmly before showing me to my first lecture class of the day. She enters the lecture hall before me, going to speak to the teacher, who luckily hasn't started yet.

I catch a glimpse of Khazon sitting close to a girl in the front row; His eyes blaze fury as he looks at me, and I smirk, waving at him.

"My name is Mr. Rickman," the teacher says, holding his hand out and drawing my attention back to him.

I glance down at it before taking it. He balls a fist with his other hand before throwing it at me.

Miss Shay squeals beside us and rushes to leave.

I dodge, twisting his wrist in my hand, sending him to his knees until he taps the desk. I let him go. "Sorry, sir."

"No. Perfect. You shouldn't be able to trust anyone besides your team. Everyone in this world is out for you, and people want to trick you. You have good reflexes. How?"

"Club life," I admit. "People try to get handsy."

He lets out a chuckle. "Yeah. Human men tend to do it the most. Take a seat anywhere, Asura. It's a pleasure to have you here."

Smiling, I peek at the open seat right behind Khazon. As I walk back to my chair, I feel something flying, and I sidestep as the ball flies and hits the wall. I sidestep as the ball flies and hits the wall.

"I'll get you one day," Mr. Rickman says, pointing at me as I take my seat.

"Oh, I'm sure you will, sir."

He scoffs, turns to the board, and begins drawing on it. "To be a Soul Reaper, you must accomplish a few things. One, you have to channel your telum, which is the weapon you will use every time you hunt a soul. Souls help our shadow realm, and the underworld runs smoother. They power anything and everything. From the lights to the cars. Earth runs on Dunkin; we run on souls." He leans on his desk.

The room is quiet as I glance around, smirking. The room is filled with supernatural beings of all ages, all wearing red like me. Demons, fae, orcs, shifters— you name it. Anyone can technically be a Soul Reaper.

"Two, look for your three hellhounds. Pick someone you can trust and who you think will protect you. You have to learn to work with them. You must learn to work with them and work as a team, so pick someone you trust the most." A hand raises from a girl who looks familiar, but I can't place it.

"Yes?" the teacher asks.

"When's the ceremony for both?

"So, the telum ceremony is this Friday for the new recruits. The higher levels, like Khazon here and Miya, run it."

The girl next to Khazon twists around, waving as if we care about who the fuck she is. I certainly do not.

"Bonding ceremony happens when you get your hounds. From there, you set up with Dean Moon to book the field for it."

My head spins with questions, so I raise my hand like a good girl.

"Yes."

"So, how do you get hellhounds to join you?"

He shrugs. "Sometimes it's as simple as asking. "Sometimes, it's as simple as asking, and sometimes it might take the telum ceremony to show that you are strong. Any way you can get someone to trust you, you can do it." I glance at Khazon, who looks annoyed and stiff. The Miya girl seems comfortable, having her hands on his biceps and leaning into him. I raise my hand again, "Sir, say someone else has the hellhound you want—"

Khazon whips his head around quickly. "Don't you dare!"

49

I bite my lip to stop the smirk from spreading across my face. "Shush, Khazon. I'm asking a question."

"I'm assuming you were going to ask," Mr. Rickman says, clearing his throat, "what should you do if someone has a hound you want? If the hound agrees, you can 'steal.'"

"Interesting," I say with a wide smirk on my face. Khazon does not look happy at all.

# Asura

"Don't you dare steal my hound!" Khazon finally explodes as soon as we both step out into the hall. His face is red through his tan skin, and his finger is in my face.

I push it away, ignoring the unwanted attention from the supernatural beings around us. "Calm it down, Khazzie. I was just kidding."

Khazon sighed, probably realizing that I didn't want Ledger. "This is not a game, Asura. Hellhounds protect, and I trust mine and *only* mine."

I smirk. "Oh, I trust him too."

He growls like a hellhound.

That Miya girl moves beside Khazon and hooks her arm around his. "Come on, baby. Let's leave the trash where she belongs."

My jaw drops, but I'm almost smiling. "Trash, huh? Cute."

She snarls at me, pushing her hair over her horns.

"Yeah, Khazzie. Wouldn't want to be seen around *trash*." I mock her voice before snorting. "Stupid bitch," I say, moving to walk away.

"Excuse me?!" I hear the shriek behind me.

I ignore her, looking down at my paper to get to the next class. I hear her huffing and puffing, but I know she'd never dare to hit me from behind. I thought we were over the high school drama.

Someone moves beside me, the girl who looked familiar with her hand raised in class. "Do you like to make enemies on your first day?"

I scoff. "She can get in line; I have a long waiting list for a piece of this ass."

"Do you remember me?"

"Of course, I do..." I glance at her, narrowing my eyes.

She chuckles, making me look up at her. Her pale skin sits so well with her blazing red hair. Her eyes are dark, almost black. "Weird, we actually never met, so I don't know how you'd remember me. But you've met my dad."

"Hades?"

She shakes her head, curls falling everywhere.

"Lucifer? Although I don't think he has a daughter... Neither does Hades..."

"Grim Reaper."

I gasp. "You're the Grim Reaper's daughter?"

She leans in, smirking. "So is Miya."

My face scrunches up in disgust. "Well...How is your dad? I miss him!"

She smirks. "He's good! You haven't missed much."

"I'm Asura." I hold out my hand.

She chuckles. "I know. I'm Amos." I take her in once more. She doesn't look like Grim, more like his wife, which makes sense. Miya is blonde like Grim and kind of ugly like him, too. At least Amos got her mother's look. *Thank the gods.*

"What class do you have next?" I ask.

"I have weapon defenses and then self-defense."

I glance down at my classes. "Same. Lead the way."

The gym looks like an average high school gym, but there seem to be pairs fighting with each other already, poles in hand.

The teacher walks up to me as we enter the class after changing into shorts and short-sleeved shirts. "You're new. How good are you with weapons, girl?"

I shrug. "It's Asura, and I don't think I'm good. But I think my reflexes and hand-eye coordination are good." *From years of falling flat on my face from the pole.*

"We will see. You will learn how to use different types of weapons in his class until you get your telum. Let's get started."

The teacher, Mrs. Hill, worked with us all. She taught me a bit about how to use weapons to my advantage. I got the hang of it, but something I struggle with is trying to figure out how someone is going to react to my hits, and I tend not to block. Amos had fun whacking me in the head a few times. We're sitting on the mats, waiting for the next class to start; luckily, it's in the same room.

"Do you have hounds?" I ask Amos, leaning onto my hands.

"Two. A telepathic hound named Snow, and his brother, Goethe, who is a telekinetic hound."

I nod. "That's so cool. How did you… recruit them? I'm very unsure how you get someone to join in with you or even how to talk to them."

"Well, we've all been friends for a while, so it just kind of worked."

"The only hellhounds I've known were Hades's," I say with a groan. The room chills and my back stiffens, causing me to look up. A tall, handsome guy strolls into the gym; His black hair is down, falling against his forehead.

*What are they feeding these boys?*

His dark blue eyes move to me because I'm staring and maybe... drooling? His lips are in a frown, and his dark features are in the same fashion. His strong jaw tightens as he lifts his chin slightly.

My eyes trickle lower to his crotch: gray sweats and a white long-sleeved shirt. Gray sweats are my weakness; Any sweats that show a clear outline of a dick are my weakness. *And his is…*

"Asura?" Amos mutters beside me.

My eyes stay glued on him as he passes us. He pries his eyes from me before walking toward the bleachers against the wall.

My eyes lower to his ass.

*How fucking sexy…*

Amos hits my shoulder. "You're drooling."

I blink, turning away and back to her. "Oh, the things I'd do to him."

She giggles. "You don't even know him!"

"I don't need to know him. He's fucking hotter than hell."

"He's a hellhound."

I groan. "All hellhounds better not be this hot."

She leans in. "I think he's an ice hellhound… He might not have a reaper, and he doesn't talk to anyone but a few people."

"Cold, brooding, and hot… My type of man."

Oh, are we talking about me, baby?" I hear Ledger's voice before he slams down onto the mat next to us. His red eyes on me.

I cock a brow. "Yeah, you too. But mainly tall, dark, and handsome in the corner."

Ledger's eyes move to the corner, and a frown comes on his face. "Inarian? You think he's hot?"

I nod. *Inarian.*

"He's not. He's actually the opposite. Cold."

"Does he have a reaper?"

He crosses his arms over his chest, and I notice the way his muscles bulge around his biceps. *Hellhounds might be the death of me.* "I don't know, and don't care. The guy's a dick; You don't want him as a hound."

I glance at Amos. "I'm missing something, aren't I?"

"Nope. Just a douchebag of a guy," Ledger answers.

*Like I need to know Inarian's personality while I'm riding his face; All I need are his tongue, dick, and fingers.* I smirk at my joke, earning a glare from Ledger as if he could read my mind.

"You can find better hounds than him."

I huff, crossing my arms over my chest. "We shall see."

Mrs. Hill, the fight instructor, moves out, clapping her hands. "All right. Today we are going to try combat training; Pick someone of the opposite size to spar with."

I look up at Ledger, but Amos grabs his arm first. "Sorry, I'm not working with anyone else. Go get your iceman."

Ledger and I lock eyes. He looks like he wants to murder Amos as his crimson eyes deepen a shade.

To my luck, Inarian is one of the last available people. I walk to him, and our eyes lock halfway, and I can't read his expression at all. "Want to be my partner?" I chirp.

He stares at me and then shrugs.

"Okay…" Amos *did* say that he barely talks to anyone.

"Okay! Line up on a mat," Mrs. Hill instructs.

We both move to our spots, and I feel eyes burning into me. I glance over to see Ledger staring at us. His jaw is tight, but I can't tell why he's pissed. *Is it… jealousy?*

"Now, in some situations, you'll have a tall hellhound and a short reaper," Mrs. Hill says, pointing at Inarian and me as an example. I wasn't short in the Earthbound world, but amongst hounds, I'm short. "The short and small might not be the strongest, but they could be the fastest and agile. Vice versa, the tall and big might be slow, but their punches are powerful. You have to use things to your advantage. Let's begin with jabs and where to hit them."

I lean forward but look up to Inarian. "I'm Asura."

He cocks a dark brow before moving across from me and preparing to jab at me.

"I know your name. Inarian. Do you like to be called Inari or Nari?"

He puts his fingertips against my chest. My brows pull together, watching him. In a quick motion, he makes a fist and pushes it into my chest without even reeling back.

57

I gasp, grabbing my chest as I fall to my ass. I swear I feel my heart skip a beat or two, not in a good way. I rub the tender spot, looking up at him. That's going to leave a mark. Once I'm able to catch my breath, I roll to my knees before standing, "Damn, okay. No ni-nicknames, ass."

He smirks, motioning for me to hit him with a gesture to his chest.

I move to him, coming up to the start of his chest. I hate to admit that he's slightly taller than Ledger. I make a fist, curling my thumb around my closed fingers before reeling back and hitting his sternum.

Instead of him hurting or groaning, I yelp, pulling back my hand and shaking it. "Motherfucker!"

That one fucking punch lands me in the nurse's office, getting my already bruising knuckles checked out. I have to get used to the pain because I'm sure this is going to happen more, especially since Mrs. Hill is keeping us as partners.

The nurse wraps it, earning a groan from me. "Try not to punch any more walls."

I smile. "I'll heal fast. I'm the daughter of the Devil."

She smiles back. "I guess so. But still don't need you going home with a broken fist, darling."

I lean in. "What's your name?"

"Mrs. Goldie," the old lady says.

"Asura."

She waves me off, standing. "I know you. Stay away from walls, darling."

I snort. *Unless the wall is named Inarian.*

# Ledger

I push Inarian as soon as we enter the locker room after class, feeling the cold touch my hot hands. "You really had to go that hard, ass?"

He cocks a brow. "Aw. Did I hurt your girlfriend? Sorry."

I roll my eyes. "Next time, don't be such a fucking dickhead, ice boy."

"Fuck off, flame breather," he scoffs. "I'm not going to baby your girlfriend. The last time I checked, she's my partner, and I've been tasked with teaching her how to fight. *You* should have picked her if you wanted her so badly." He moves away.

His words anger me. He just never keeps his mouth shut. I bite my tongue and clench my fist. "Hurt her again, and I'm fucking you up, *Nari.*"

Inarian smirks in my face. "*Mad,* I might get this girl's pussy first, too? I'll tell you how it tastes, *Ledge.*"

Anger rises inside me, and I can't help but react instead of think.

# Asura

Amos moves from the wall, curls bouncing as she walks my way into the hall.

I smile a bit. "Waited for me?"

"You got lunch like me, don't you?" She leads the way out to the academy lobby, where a massive sign with the academy's name sits against the wall of the stairs. I follow her outside, admiring the structure of the enormous academy. She leads us to a building my brother labeled a mess hall. "How's your wrist?" Amos asks.

I shrug. "I didn't need to go to the nurse for it. But hitting Inarian was like hitting fucking bricks. He didn't even talk to me the whole time. How am I supposed to find out if that hellhound has a reaper?"

She snorts. "Just ask me; I know all the ins and outs because of Miya."

I cock a brow as we enter the beige brick building. "So, does he?"

She smirks, knowing what she's doing. "Does he *what*?"

"Does he have a reaper, you ass?" I push her with my good hand.

The mess hall is set up like an average college-looking cafeteria. Well, as average as it can be with gray or red demons running around and seven-foot-tall hellhounds shouting to each other. Khazon passes us with his other two hellhounds. His hounds are dressed in black uniforms, usually assigned to hellhounds, while reapers wear red.

Khazon's eyes meet mine but lower to see the ice wrap around my fist. His jaw tightens, but he continues.

I groaned, throwing the ice out in the nearest trash bin.

Amos chuckles. "Trouble in lover paradise?"

I roll my eyes. "Khazzie is my bestie, not my lover; He just doesn't know that we are best friends."

"He changed after you left."

I lick my lips, moving to the first line with Amos. "Well, he needs to just… you know, suck it the fuck up. We've been best friends since birth, and now he's dating some bitch, and he thinks he's big shit." I freeze, looking at Amos. "Sorry…At least you don't have a shit name or your father's looks."

She snorts. "I agree; she's a bitch. Mom named her. Dad named me."

I smirk, grabbing an apple, sandwich, and energy drink. They have a lot of Earthbound brands here, and I'm not going to ask about the trouble they go through to get it. I get to the line to pay, shoving the apple into my mouth and pulling out my wallet.

"Oh...no," the lady says. "It's free for the Devil and Grim Reaper's daughters."

I cock a brow, staring at her before pulling out a few hell coins and putting them in her hand.

Amos does the same, and we walk to an open table near the corner. "I hate the free treatment; Nothing is ever free in this world," she says.

I set my stuff down, taking my apple out of my mouth, almost drooling. I open my mouth to speak to Amos just as some reaper pops down next to me, holding out a hundred-dollar bill. "How much to get the dance that Ledger got? This cover it?"

Cocking a brow, I stare at him. He's not ugly by any means, but I'm not in the mood, and I'm definitely not giving him a lap dance here. I take the hundred, putting it in my bra, but turning back to Amos. "Okay, you never answered my question about Inarian."

Amos clamps her hand over her mouth to stop herself from laughing.

"What about my dance?" the guy whines.

"What about it, little boy?" I snap.

He cocks a brow. "I'm not little, baby. Give me a chance to show it."

I laugh in his face. "As if. Bye."

His face morphs into anger quickly as his demon begins to form. "*My* money?"

I smirk. "There's a fee to talk to me, little boy. Fuck out of my face before I let *my* demon out." The scariest type of people are those who can't handle rejection, and I dealt with many of them at the club.

He stands up, making the chair fall to the ground before he moves away. "*Fucking* bitch."

I laugh, waving him away. "God. Even demon men think they have the audacity to be dicks."

Amos lets out a chuckle. "It's Andrew."

My brow bounces. *Huh?*

"Spreading that rumor that Ledger got a dance from you for a hundred dollars."

I smirk. "Not a rumor, but I think it's because he needed my scent to follow me."

"So, you were a stripper in the Earthbound world? How was that?" Amos asks.

I nod. "It had its ups and downs. Quick money, though." I glance behind Amos, locking eyes with a guy in the far corner of the room. He has a mask with chains over his mouth and nose, leaving his bright lime-green eyes visible. He leans forward, chains jiggling and swinging. He's in all black, just like his messy shoulder-length hair. His hands move to the table, and I see he has gloves on them.

63

Amos follows my gaze before leaning forward. "That's Saw, a toxic hellhound."

I smirk. "I happen to love toxic men."

He cocks his brow as if he can hear me. Honestly, if he's a hound, he probably did. They have the ability to smell and hear anything.

She snorts. "No, he's not a toxic man. I mean... he might be. But he's a—"

Before she can say anything, he moves and lifts his mask slightly. Then I see liquid running from under his mask, his spit dripping from his lips. I let out a small gasp, and heat runs through me as my core clenches. *What can I say: I love spit?* But instantly, the saliva starts to hiss as it burns through the wood.

"Oh, fuck me," I say with a smirk, watching his toxic spit sizzle out. "How much of his spit would it take to hurt me? Is it enough to at least get me off first?"

His brows rose as if he didn't know this was how I would act.

"Oh, please, you knew what you did, hound," I say in a low voice. He and every other hound probably smelled my arousal the instant it happened.

He sits back against the wall. His green eyes crinkle as if he has a smirk under his mask.

My pussy throbs. Human men seem... selfish. I mean, demons are, too. But human men just want to come instead of making me come. So, I am always left unsatisfied.

Rune Hunt

"Jigsaw sticks to himself; He's a second-year hound with no reaper."

I look at Amos. "Lucky me." But when I look back at Jigsaw, he rolls his lime-green eyes. I can't help but smile. Between him and Inarian, I have a challenge. Of course, I want the hellhounds that don't want me, but I'm always up for challenges. "Inarian?"

"Free for any reaper. But both guys have denied the multiple offers they've got."

I bite into my apple just as a tall, tan hound blocks my view of Saw by sitting right across from him. My eyes wander down his broad back, and then I take in the curls on the top of his head.

"Can we talk?" Khazon says, making me jolt and look to the side. I didn't even hear him get so close since I had been focused on men more than my surroundings.

"You need a bell," I tease.

"Come on," Khazon says, moving without me.

I share a look with Amos before grabbing my drink and apple, following Khazon. Miya is sitting with his hellhounds; arms crossed at her chest. I wave, smirking as her thin lips curl into a deeper frown.

"What are you doing here for real, Asura?" Khazon asks as soon as we get outside the mess hall.

I smirk, throwing my apple away in the nearest trash bin. "You don't like me being at the academy?"

"No," he says firmly. "Your father hired me to bring you home just to let you out again?"

I smile. "He thinks being a reaper would benefit me as the heir."

He leans against the back of a bench. "I thought you didn't want to be the heir."

I shrug. "Formalities, Khazzie."

"Stop calling me that."

My brows pull together. "Tell your girlfriend not to call me trash. Thanks for coming to my aid, by the way."

He cocks a brow. "You need me now? You're a grown-ass woman. Fight your own battles."

I scoff, looking up at him. "Are you really that pissed I left?"

He shakes his head. "Fuck no. Why would I? I don't care what you do. Leave again. I might even get paid to get your dumbass again."

I scoff. "My ass is brilliant. Thank you very much. Don't let Miya find out that you're talking about my ass."

He glares at me. "Just stay out of my way and stay away from Ledger. You're already getting him in trouble."

My brows pull together as I look up at him. "Huh?"

He rolls his eyes. "Ledger fought with Inarian, and both got into trouble."

My brows pull together. "Why would he do that?"

Khazon shrugs. "He wants pussy. I don't fucking know. Maybe he just fought him to fight him.

66

But if I find out it's because you hurt your little hand on Inarian, I'm going to be pissed. My hellhounds are in line before you."

I scoff. "Fuck you, dick! I've been here for one day; I promise it's not because Ledger wants me. He does want me, though; Lots of men do."

He steps closer, jaw tightening. "And you are proud of that? You are proud that you used to get half naked for money?"

I cock a brow. "No, but I'm not ashamed either. You can't make me feel ashamed for being comfortable with stuff you men do either way. I make money from men who willingly come and watch me; It's not on me that they showed up."

"It's about respect."

"To whom? Because I respect myself, and I'm so much more comfortable in my body and with my skills, Khazzie," I say. "Check yourself. You're acting like my boyfriend."

He stares down at me. Although he's not a hellhound, he's at least a foot above me, and still, I smirk up at him. "Don't call me—"

"Khazzie. Got it, Khazzie. I'll see you around!" I push him back and wave him off just as a group of people comes out of the doors. It's time to go to the next class.

I spend the following four classes alone with no one I know, and I don't care to talk to anyone. During the last period, the lady from the office, Miss Shay, drops off the key to my dorm and the room number.

Hell's Reaper

The campus is set up with the academy front and center, with the mess hall to the left side of it. The academy is filled with training fields, then all four dorms arch around the academy and end with the library.

I slide my key into the door when I make it to my room in the reaper dorms as a few jock-looking reapers pass, all eyeing me. I hear their whispers about my ass. I roll my eyes, opening the door. The dorm looks like a suite with a small living room and kitchen area. There are four doors, two on each side of the room.

I move to the other room on the right-hand side. The space inside is a pretty decent size, with a full-size bed, dresser, and desk. I throw my bag down before pulling out my phone. The Shadow World has service, but Hell does not. I can't even call my father to see how he is.

I pull up my brother's name, Killian, and text him.

**Me:** What are you up to?

He answers almost instantly.

**Kill:** Aw, does the future Queen of Hell have no friends?

I smirk. *The cocky bastard.*

**Me:** I was just checking in on my little brother.

**Kill:** I'm eighteen now, A. But if you must know, I'm hanging with my hounds and their friends. Do you want to go somewhere to eat in the Shadow World?

I jump from the bed. It's almost hard to believe that Killian is eighteen years old now, and I feel like he's still the baby I used to push around. Derrick is twenty like I am, only two months younger than me; He was very close to getting the throne before me.

**Me:** If you insist.

About twenty minutes after our text exchange, I leave my empty dorm behind to meet my brother by the entrance gate. I see him talking to Ledger as we get closer.

I smile. "Hey, fighter," I tease, punching Ledger's hot arm.

He raises a brow, looking over at me. "This is who you invited, Killian?"

I cross my arms over my chest. "*You* can always stay behind."

"I was the one who came up with this!" he says, smirking and pointing to himself.

"Aw! Do you actually have ideas?" I gasp dramatically. "And thoughts?"

Ledger rolls his eyes, smiling. "Whatever, princess. Come on before we leave you behind."

# Ledger

Watching Asura struggle with chopsticks makes me laugh. She looks up at me with a frown on her face. "Do you know how to do this?" she questions.

I stare at her momentarily, taking in her glaring brown eyes. Her eyes are a dark chocolate color with a hint of blood red. She's a demon for sure, although I've never seen her demon form. Before the mission, Khazon said that if she shifted, let her go because there's no way we would have been able to beat her. Could you picture that? Three of the most substantial level hellhounds and the Angel of Death cannot defeat one girl?

I use the chopsticks to pick up a sushi piece and dip it into the soy sauce before eating it.

Asura rolls her eyes. "Yeah. Yeah. Expert."
She tries again, pushing her silver hair behind her ear.

I let out a groan, reaching over to her.
Conversations around us with Killian and his hounds
continue as if we aren't even here. "No. No." I take my
time fixing her fingers to where they should be. "Like
this." Her hands soften but don't take the form I am
trying to teach her.

I look up to see her watching my face. We lock
eyes, and for some reason, I swallow hard. I'm
touching the Princess of Hell. I pull back, sitting up.
She's royalty here in the Shadow World, but she
doesn't feel like it by how she acts. She feels like an
ordinary everyday girl, but clearly, she isn't. Not that
she's much different than any girls I've met. Her dad
just so happens to be the Devil that can smite me for
even breathing the same air as her.

"Why did you fight Inarian?" she questions
after a moment.

I glance at the others who could care less about
what we're talking about. "He's a dick."

"Is that it?"

When I lick my lips, I see her dark eyes
dropping to my lips. Don't worry about it."

She cocks a dark brow, leaning in. "So, you
didn't hit him because I hurt myself on his body?
Because that… would be stupid."

I set down my chopsticks. "Would it be,
though?"

Her lips curl into a smile. "You don't have to protect me, Ledger. I'm capable of doing it myself."

My brows pull together. "Oh, are you? So, why did I risk my life to save you from the Blood Clan?"

"Oh, please." She scoffs, stabbing the sushi with a fork and shoving it into her mouth. "I've dealt with Draco and his men before."

"How did that turn out?" I pick up my food and eat it.

"Bloody," she says after a pause.

My eyes flicker up to her. She's looking down at her food, and regret runs across her face. Asura has a reputation for hurting men who were sent after her; each time, they came back hurt and crying about her true form. Now, Khazon is getting the reputation of "Best Reaper" because we were able to bring her back, but she didn't put up too much of a fight. "I'm curious, Asura."

She looks up at me.

"Why and how did you become a..." My voice falters when I look over at her brother. *He might not know yet.*

"A stripper?" she says with a smirk.

I let out a chuckle. "I'm just curious. You probably could have used your magic and coerced men to give you money or a fancy place to stay."

She sips her drink. "What fun is that, Ledger? I grew up in the Earthbound world, and the experience was fun. Girls were always nice and made me feel like family, and it was also a way for me to get quick money."

I want to ask her if she gave men lap dances as she did for me, but I'd rather not know. It doesn't matter, and it shouldn't matter. Now, she's mine. No man will ever lay their fingers on her without me being ready to hurt them—like Inarian. Just the thought of him hurting her makes me ten degrees hotter. "Do you miss it?"

She nods. "I'd like to go back one day. It was fun, and I made friends. We would go out to clubs, dance, and drink. I had fun, even if I had to always move around to different clubs and things."

"You made friends?" I choke on my sushi. "How?"

She scoffs, but she's smirking. "With my winning personality, asshole."

I snort. "You have a personality? I thought it was just your looks."

She kicks my foot lightly. "Ass!" But when her laughter fills the air, my throat tightens. Fuck, she's so fucking beautiful, but Khazon would kill me if I took it further. That is his best friend...Or *ex*-best friend now. I'm not sure what's going on with that situation.

We all enjoy the night, drinking and overeating sushi. Asura *kind of* got the hang of using the chopsticks until she got pissed and would use her hands. Oddly enough, she's very affectionate around her brother, hugging him and tousling his hair.

Killian doesn't object, even though he's usually not affectionate.

After a while, we move to the front and pay before leaving. Asura bumps me just as we make it outside. "Thanks," she mutters, but I'm not exactly sure why she's saying it.

Killian and his three hellhounds walk ahead of us. I know two of them, but the girl is new. She's short compared to typical size hounds, and I can't tell what her power is, but I can tell she's a hellhound. Killian seems to like her, flirting the whole time.

"How did you and Khaz become partners?" Asura breaks my train of thought.

I cock a brow, shoving my hands back in my pockets. "I wouldn't call us partners."

"What do you mean? I thought the bond between a hellhound and the reaper was a partnership."

I shrug. It didn't feel like that. Khazon tells us what to do, and we listen. Sometimes it's okay, like telling us to protect Asura or to use my hell fire. But sometimes it's something like don't talk to certain people or don't look at Miya for too long. He seems very insecure, and I can see why now.

*Asura broke his heart.*

I'm not exactly sure what happened to them before, but I can tell Khazon is hurt by it.

"Hopefully, it changes for you, and I think it should be more of a partnership than a mastership," she says.

That will be a first for anyone. Reapers treat us like we are replaceable, which in a sense, we are. There are millions of hellhounds with all different types of powers. If I were to die right now, Khazon would replace me in a few days; It's how it works.

Asura stares at the small car that we piled into before. She stayed close to me the whole ride here and away from Killian's horny hellhounds.

"It's a nice night, huh?" I say before looking up at the night sky.

The Shadow World is a carbon copy of Earth. Most of the buildings are built the same way, with the same millions of windows. There are cities and countries, but we are in one of the most known city areas. Parts of this city remind me of New York: huge skyscrapers, always alive at night, and a million flashing signs to catch your attention. I wasn't on Earth a lot in my life, only the few times my mother would take us. New York was my brother's favorite place; He loved the various foods and all the different people we met.

Asura nods, looking up at the neon lights of the Japanese restaurant we were just in. For a moment, Asura reminds me of someone I once knew...Their long silver curls bounced in the breeze that surrounded us. Their dark eyes light up in the shapes of the neon signs while their beautiful skin glows. But Asura's is deep golden honey. Her pink lips are full and look kissable...

75

I blink. I barely know this girl, yet here I am, thinking about how I could bruise her lips with mine. Her attitude… It just reminds me of… *her*. She was always so confident and always so witty and kept people smiling. Asura does the same thing.

Sadness washes over me.

I won't let anything happen to her. "Can I walk you back? It's like a fifteen-minute walk… it's not far." I finally ask.

Her eyes flicker to me as a smirk runs across her face. "I guess…Might as well."

Killian looks up at us, waiting for us to move to the car.

"We are going to walk back. Don't wait up." I nod to them.

Killian cocks a brow, looking between his sister and me. "Don't do anything stupid…"

Asura snorts. "I should say the same to you, Killie."

His brows pull together.

My eyes move to Raven, his newest hound, getting in the driver's seat. Killian catches on quickly, the ivory skin on his cheeks turning red. Killian's skin is like his father's, while Asura got blessed with her mother's golden skin.

"Make sure you wrap it up," she teases, punching his arm.

"Stop it," he snaps for the first time, but I can tell he's not pissed even then. I've seen Killian mad and how hard and cold he is in his demon form, but somehow Asura gets a different side of him. More affectionate.

"Bye, Killie!" Asura waves him off.

Killian mutters under his breath for her to "fuck off," but I can see the smile on his lips.

Asura and I take our time walking to the academy. Her eyes always watch all the buildings surrounding us. I look down at her, watching her. "It's almost more beautiful than it is on Earth," she says with a small smile.

"Yeah?"

She looks up, meeting my eyes.

*I want her to be mine. I want to protect her from anyone and everyone. I want to be the one she comes to when she needs something. I want to be hers...*

"What?" She cocks a brow.

I shake my head. "Nothing."

*Asura*

I used to see Soul Reaper Stations and was amazed. My eyes would be wide, and I'd bounce around, holding my father's hand. He'd laugh at me and introduce me to those who work under him and their hounds.

## Hell's Reaper

From then on, I've always wanted to be a reaper. I want to be just as good as my father was.

I still feel the same after seeing Soul Reaper Station a few streets from the restaurant. All the feelings hit me like a brick wall, and butterflies fill my stomach. My father's vision has me on edge. He was cryptic with his vision, but I feel like he might know what's in store for me. One of the tasks of becoming a Soul Reaper is having a team I can trust. My father accomplished a lot when his hellhounds were alive, and they were loyal to him.

My eyes run over the dark building that looks like a metal cube with a vast, black metal gate surrounding it. It's mainly like that because demons have tried blowing it up, and it's made to shut down and lock everyone in or out completely. It has the same gothic feel as the academy does.

"Stop him!" a heavy voice yells, and doors slam open just as we walk past the opening of the gate of the station.

Ledger and I both turn just as someone pushes us apart. Magic shifts around me, making the whole world spin like a top. Whatever supernatural being just touched me is powerful. I reach out for something other than the ground, but I can't even tell which way the earth is. An arm wraps around my waist, and chains clank loudly as they fly past my head.

"I got him!" the same voice says, and it happens to belong to the person holding onto me.

Rune Hunt

My palms press against a hard chest as I try to push away. The arm wraps tighter around me, causing me to press against the person more. My hands reach up and grab his shoulders, trying to steady myself. "Who the fuck—what the fuck—"

"Calm down," he whispers softly. "He's a vitiligo demon. You can't stand by yourself."

"And yet," Ledger growls from somewhere on my right, "I-I have no one holding me up."

I blink, finally seeing shapes clearer. The world around me is slowly stilling itself. I can see a handsome Soul Reaper staring down at him within minutes.

"Hi," he whispers, pink eyes scanning my face. His fangs on the top and bottom of his teeth flash at me when he smiles. His short hair is just as powder pink as his eyes, falling against his forehead. A fleshy pink scar runs over his tan face, from cheek to cheek. He straightens us, pulling me up with his free hand. I grab onto his shoulders once again, feeling his warmth against me more. I've never felt so… helpless with a man before. I need him to stand.

His telum flashes at me, it's a whip with ropes of chains and spikes on end. But on the end of his whip, an ugly-looking blue demon is tied up.

"Alexis," the pink-haired fae calls over his shoulder, barely looking away. A large guy is suddenly there, towering over us. "Take him in."

The angry guy nods and moves, grabbing the telum and taking the demon back in. Only hellhounds can touch their Soul Reaper's telum. That was his hellhound?

"Are you okay?" the fae says to me.

"I'm great," Ledger says. "Hands off of the princess."

The fae looked down and quickly removed his hand from my waist, but I didn't mind. He straightens the black tactical suit that fits him well. He's in a skintight black shirt, bulletproof vest, and tight-fitted cargo pants. His pink eyes move up at Ledger. "Oh, hi, Ledger!"

*Ledger knows this fae?* My eyes stay on the guy. His body is large and wide, almost as much as Ledger's, and I can see his bulging muscles through his tactical reaper gear. He's definitely not as tall and isn't much taller than I am.

"Hi, Ryker," Ledger deadpans.

The fae, Ryker, is between us. "Oh, are you on a date with Ledger?"

I shake my head. "No."

"So, you are single?"

I nod.

Ryker leans against the gate that surrounds the station. "Very interesting…"

Cocking a brow, I lick my lips. His pink eyes drop to my lips.

"Stop it, asshole. We have to go," Ledger growls.

I chuckle, prying my eyes from the beautiful man in front of me. "See you around… Ryker, is it?"

80

Ryker flashes his fangs. "Nice meeting you, Princess Asura."

I hate being called princess. Most mean it disrespectfully, while loyal subjects mean it; it makes me uncomfortable. I certainly don't feel like the heir or a princess. But...when Ryker said it, my core grew warmer. First week back in Hell and the Shadow World, and I'm just catching up on all the hot men I've been missing out on before I get to work. I move away with Ledger before he rips Ryker apart. "What was that?" I whisper.

Ledger's jaw tightens. "Stay away from Ryker."

My brows pull together. "Or?"

"Asura..." he growls, making my core tighten. "Drop it and forget about Ryker; He's not a good guy."

*And you are?* Biting my tongue, I watch him walk ahead of me.

We walk a few more minutes, getting closer to the academy. Ledger hasn't said anything since his warning, but I know the type of men he and Ryker are; They are the type of men that won't settle down with one person.

I'm not that type of woman, either. My mind drifts back to all the handsome men I've met this week alone: Ledger, Jigsaw, the toxic hound, Inarian, the ice hound, and now Ryker, the high-level Soul Reaper.

I can't even imagine settling down with one of them or making them settle down with me. What did settling down mean? Would Ledger and I get married, have kids, and a white picket fence? That's not what I want or need from life. Men aren't my priority; Being the best queen, I can be is.

"Look who we have here." A voice almost has me jolting.

Both of us twist around to the voice.

It was the guy who gave me a hundred dollars during lunch to give him a lap dance. I roll my eyes and begin walking again, but one of the guys steps in my way.

"Desi," Ledger growls. "Why are you here?"

I feel the hand of another running down my back. I stiffen, pulling myself flush against Ledger. I don't need protection but feeling unsafe around men stirs something in me.

*Unleash me…* that beautiful voice in my head says. My jaw tightens, and anger that might not entirely be mine rises.

"Your little girlfriend here owes me a lap dance," Desi says, head tilting as he looks down at me.

Ledger steps between us, his heat blazing against my skin. He's mad; his heat alone made the gym room slightly hotter when I was fighting with Inarian. "You fucking touch her again, and I'll beat the living shit out of you."

My wide eyes look up at him. I can only stare at the back of him, seeing a soft scar coming from the back of his jacket. I barely know Ledger; we just met. What kind of man would beat someone up for me? I've…never had someone even say that to anyone. I'm used to men touching me without consent. Well, I should be used to it.

"Stay out of this, low-level hound. This is reaper business," another one of the friends says.

Ledger's shoulders widen in defense. "If any of you touch her, I promise I'll kill you."

*Kill? That ensures getting into trouble, and neither of us needs that right now.* I remember what Khazon said, and Ledger can't get into any more trouble. With wide eyes, I grab Ledger's hips. "Let's just go." He slowly moves away from the three Soul Reapers with me clinging to his back.

A hand wraps around my bicep and pulls on me until my chest hits another. The other hand wraps around my throat. A raspy gasp escapes my throat.

Before I can even think about striking back, heat rushes past my face and lands against Desi's face. His hold on me loosens, and I stumble back.

Looking up, I see Ledger standing over Desi. Steam is rolling off his shoulder with each deep breath he takes. "I told you not to touch my girl."

My heart skips a beat. *His girl?*

Desi scrambles to his feet, already thinking about his next move. "You will stand down, hound. Before I get you and your reaper into trouble."

"Ledge," I warn, but he doesn't even seem to hear me. His crimson eyes are locked on his target.

"As a higher-level reaper, you will listen to me. Leave, Ledger... Leave the girl."

Ledger's eyebrows pull together. "You're fucking sick if you think I would ever leave her with three fucking rapists like you guys."

Desi's brows bounce as if he's offended by the word "rapist."

"What did you call me? Watch your mouth. We don't need your reputation getting worse than what it is."

I glance at Ledger's back. *What does he mean?*

It's silent for a moment before Ledger speaks over his shoulder at me, "Go back to the academy, Asura."

I step forward.

"Go!" he barks, and I return to that step. In a way, I understand. If Ledger sees me as a thing he wants to protect, I am a weakness, and his head will be on a swivel with all three men surrounding us.

However, I am far from a weakness.

My eyes scan one of the guys that are with Desi. He looks like he's calculating something until he finally reaches for me.

Ledger tenses, but I'm ready. I kick upwards, balling my fist for protection. My boots connect with his jaw, drawing spit from his mouth. Before I can even think, the other two attacks. Desi launches himself at Ledger. I punch out at the other guy, but he dodges, grabbing my throat.

My jaw clenches.

*Hurt him…* the voice in my head whispers so lightly, it feels like wind blowing through my head.

I hook my thumb between the web of his thumb and index finger and yank my head back. My world spins at the movement, but I recover quickly.

Hell's Reaper

A fist punches the other reaper rushing at me, and I see Ledger paying attention. My eyes lock onto his body for a split second. His muscles move with each movement he makes, and each one looks more calculated than the other.

Khazon is lucky to have a hellhound that fights this skillfully.

*Crack!*

My head whips backward from a hard punch to my jaw. My ass hits the ground, and I taste iron on my tongue.

Ledger's red eyes connect with mine, and I forget about the fight for a moment. His shoulders are heaving, and his jaw is tightening with each harsh breath. Rage fills his eyes, and he looks at the guy who hit me.

I let out the air I was holding, and I looked at Desi, whose eyes widened and locked on Ledger.

"Ledger, I'm fine," I say, but my words are muffled because of the pain radiating to the left side of my jaw.

Ledger grabs the guy and, in a flash, punches him hard. We all freeze, and I am in horror, watching.

*Thud! Thud!*

The guy is on the ground now, and Ledger is punching him repeatedly. My eyes widen as blood sprays against the pavement.

I glance at Desi to tell him to stop Ledger as if he can, but the other reapers are gone, and they left their friend behind.

86

*Crack!*

The sickening noise of something cracking in the guy's body makes me jump to my feet. I grab Ledger's shoulders and pull, but he doesn't budge. Ledger's eyes are trained on where his fists are flying.

"Ledger!" I call, but his body is too strong to hold back.

Blood sprays all over us with every blow. His muscles strain, and I watch it. The guy doesn't even look like himself anymore.

I grab Ledger's jaw and yank his face to mine. His movement thank the devil, stops, and our eyes lock.

"Let's go before someone finds us."

His jaw twitches.

"You won. Let's go."

His face softens, and he whispers, "This isn't about winning. He hurt you."

My eyes scan his face. I see the fury in him and feel the heat of it against my palm. Blood splatter covers his face, and still, my eyes drop to his lips, wondering what he tastes like. I've never had a man so willing to get thrown into jail for me. I've never had a man defend me. I've never felt this safe around someone. He'd do anything to protect me without even really knowing me. "Why?"

"Why what?" Ledger whispers, standing.

"Why would you do this? Why would you be so fucking stupid?" I couldn't help the anger that rose inside me, but I didn't fully understand it.

"Asura." He groans, reaching for me.

I push away, moving from him. I half expect him to stay behind and beat the fuck out the guy more, but instead, he follows. It makes me walk faster and further away from him.

"Asura!" he says, trying to keep close to me. I can't remember exactly where I am or how to return to the academy from here, so I turn until I finally get to a dead-end alleyway. Then I feel his hot hands wrap around my bicep and pull me to a stop.

I rip myself away from him. "Don't touch me."

He steps close to me. "Are you scared of me?"

A snort escapes me. "As if. My father is the King of Hell, and I'm barely scared of him." Ledger's wraith is nothing compared to my father's.

"Then why are you running from me?"

Rage builds and shakes me to my core. "Why are you risking your chances at the academy for me?"

"Because I could care less about the fucking academy. No one touches what is mine!"

"I'm not yours!"

"Yeah." He steps closer. "You are."

I scoff. "I belong to no man."

With a heavy sigh, he runs a bloody hand over his face, smearing blood.

I swallow. Watching him fight and now covered in blood has done something to me. I feel the heat between my legs; *I've never had a man do that for me...*

His red eyes narrow on me. "Are you... turned on?" Blood is splattered all over his clothes and running down his hard face. His eyes are as red as the fire in hell, and his teeth are clenched.

"You like that I fucked someone up for you?"

I swallow hard.

He steps closer. "I would fuck anyone up to keep you safe."

I really think he would too.

His large hand wraps around my throat, and all the blood rushes to my head. My thighs clamp together, trying to relieve the aching between them. He tilts my head back up to him. Ledger is so much bigger than me, towering over my petite frame and looking down at me like I'm his fucking prey. He licks his lips as if he can taste my arousal.

His body presses me into the cold brick behind me, and he leans down until our faces are level. "No one will ever touch you again unless it's me making you come. You're mine."

Confidently and full of lust, I lift my face, a smirk running across my face. "Prove it."

*As if beating someone half to death isn't proof enough.*

Ledger grips the back of my thigh, and with one hand, he lifts me until I'm at his eye level. Before I can even think or tell him to put me down, his lips crash into mine. His heat rushes through my body, lips tasting like the wine he had for dinner. *Sweet and inviting.*

Hell's Reaper

I return the feverish energy, grabbing a fistful of his hair and kissing him back. Warmth rushes between my legs, and my core begs for more as I wrap my legs around his torso. His hand on my ass squeezes, earning a moan from me.

He grips my body feverishly as both need and desire fill me. My pussy pulsates as I roll my hips against his stomach. The abs under his shirt flex, pressing into my clit. "Fuck," I mutter. His free hand sneaks between us and rubs against my pussy.

My eyes roll back behind my closed lids. His touch is warm and demanding.

The sound of fabric shredding fills my ears, and I feel the cold against my pussy. I pull back with a gasp, looking up. "Did you just rip my pants?"

Ledger nods, blood starting to dry against his cheek. The sound of him unbuckling his belt hits my ears. My body begins getting my pussy ready for his large size. My body aches to have his warmth, to feel him close. I look down the alleyway. We are in the dark area of it, but we aren't too far from the street. "What if someone sees us?"

His hand lifts my chin to look up at him. "Good. Then they will know you're mine."

My eyes slowly widen. *Fuck. That's hot.* I barely know this guy, and I can tell he would murder for me... *Should I be worried?* I hate to say my stomach is filled with warmth as my pussy slowly gets wetter and wetter. *This shouldn't be turning me on. But what can I say? I love toxic men.*

Rune Hunt

I feel the tip of his penis against my lips, and I look between us. I knew he was big, but not this *fucking* big. His cock looks about twelve inches— maybe more—and it's wide, as thick as my fist.

"That thing isn't going to fit."

He snorts. "You don't think you can handle it?"

When I finally pry my eyes from the massive beast, I look up in time to see spit drip from his mouth right onto the tip. We lock eyes as I hear his hand jerking up and down his wet dick.

*Dear God.*

My legs are shaking with anticipation. I don't know what to do. Ledger has total control, pinning me against the building.

Then I feel his tip gliding between my lips, and I shudder.

"I'm taking what is mine, okay?"

I swallow. *Is he going to slam into me and hurt me?* I give him a nod. "So, take it. Stop talking about it."

Fear rushes through me as he lifts me a bit and aligns his tip right against my opening. Slowly, he inches in, but before he gets far, he pulls back. Inch by inch, he slowly eases himself into me. It's tight, no matter how wet my pussy is. A gasp climbs up my throat, and I feel him cease movement.

His cock pulsates inside of me, twitching. "I can stop," he whispers.

I open my eyes and look up at him, but I shake my head. I want this. My pussy is growing wetter with each inch, and my hips feel so full, even though I don't think he's entirely inside me. "Fuck, no. I thought you were going to take what's yours?"

He growls, chest rumbling against mine. He grabs my hips and lifts me from his dick and pushes me back on it.

My head drops back as pain and pleasure rush through me. He doesn't stop, finding a nice pace, and the pain is soon replaced with toe-curling pleasure. Each time he's deep inside me, my hips tighten, and moans leave my mouth.

I press my face into his neck, feeling his comforting presence.

"Fuck, you're so wet." He grabs my neck and tilts my head back. His other hand lifts me with no effort.

My eyes squint, and my heels dig into his back. "It feels so good, Ledger."

A smirk runs across his lips. "Whose pussy is this, Asura?"

"Mine," I declare with a moan.

He slams into me, now using his hips and pulling me onto his dick. I gasp. "No, it's not; It's mine."

Ledger looks crazed, blood on his body and dark red eyes on me. He slams into me harder and deeper, making me throw my head back. My thighs are shaking and giving out; I've never felt this amount of pleasure before. The orgasm that is building is almost crumbling. I grab his shoulders and help with the bouncing.

"Say it, Asura. Tell me you're mine. No one will ever touch you again."

I shake my head, unable to think. The orgasm is so close that I'm able to taste it. My hips are bucking, and my nails are digging into his shoulder. I can barely breathe with my heart pounding so hard.

"Say it, Asura, or I will stop."

*No!* "Ledger, please don't."

He growls. "Say it, *princess.*"

My pussy clenches around him. "Ledger, I-I'm so close."

"I know, baby. Your pussy is so tight, and it's getting tighter. You are so soaked for me."

"Not for you."

He grabs my throat and tightens it until all the blood is rushing to my head, and I'm crying out. "Not for me? This is my pussy."

My toes curl.

"Say it, Asura."

White dances behind my eyelids and my cries heighten.

"Now or I stop and leave—"

*No!* "It's yours, Ledger! My pussy is yours. Don't stop! Please!" The orgasm hits hard, and my pussy explodes. I arch my back, and my pussy tightens. I dig my nails into his shoulder and muffle my moans with his neck.

Moaning, he slams into me until he finally comes hard with a rumbling growl, and semen spills down my thighs. "Fuck!" He breathes hard, head dropping down.

# Ledger

"I had fun tonight, thanks," Asura whispers. "It's been a rough fucking day, that's for sure."

Glancing down at her, I see her legs shaking as she walks, even after I let her take a long breather. She has my jacket around her waist, covering the hole I made to fuck her. I can't believe only hours ago, she had a hurt hand, we went for sushi, she met that arrogant elf, I beat someone for touching her, and we fucked. I can't even call it just a fuck. Usually, I fuck girls and leave them; I'd never just leave her in that alleyway. Even on the way back and smelling her constantly, I knew I needed more. "How's your hand?"

"Bruised. But I'll get used to fighting against all the indestructible bodies in class."

I smirk. "Hellhounds tend to be a tad stronger than normal demons because we are made to protect."

A smirk runs across her lips. "Are hellhounds Cerberus's love child?"

I snort. "Love child? He isn't even a shifter. There are many more hellhounds in the Shadow World than in Hell."

She nods, pushing her hair back. "I was just curious. I'm not often in the Shadow World; I didn't even know you had sushi!" She bumps me.

"The future Queen of Hell has to stay in Hell, huh? Is that why you left?" I tease.

She looks up at me with a smirk. "No, I'm allowed to go anywhere I want to. I didn't have many friends as a kid aside from Khazon. If we did anything, it was in Hell. Like, seeing Persephone's fields and then playing with her son, Ozzy."

"How beautiful is the field?"

She looks down, shoving her hands into the pockets of her jacket. "One of the most beautiful places I've ever seen."

I smirk, staring down at her. Her eyes twinkle with the memory of it. "Better than Earthbound?"

She snorts. "Fuck yes! Although there are a lot of cool and beautiful places. I'll show you one day, and I'll show you the fields."

I lick my lips, holding the door open for her. No one has ever been that nice to me. People tend to break their promises, so I won't get my hopes up too much. I watch her ass as she walks into the Soul

Reaper's dorms and moves to the right, over toward the stairwell. Why would Khazon ever let this go? "How did you and Khazon become friends?"

She stops, looking down at me from the step she's on. "I'm the daughter of the Devil, and he's the son of Death. Our parents are kind of close."

I let out a short laugh. "Got me there." I step up a few steps so that I'm level with her. The height difference between us is almost hilarious, but it doesn't seem to bother her.

Her dark eyes flicker to my lips. I lick my lips and see that she does that same, but then she bites her lip. I move close to her, hands grabbing the railing behind her to cage her in. "Kiss me."

She scoffs, rolling her eyes. "Don't tell me what to do. I feel like you want me more."

I cock a brow. "I won't tell anyone that the Princess of Hell wants me, a low-level hellhound."

Her eyes narrow, and her brows pull together. Even mad, she looks beautiful. "Don't call yourself that. You have the power of Hell's fire."

*Does she really not think I am just a low-level hellhound?* One side of my mouth curls, but I decide to make a move. I reach up and brush my fingers against her cheek. She inhales sharply, and goosebumps rise under my touch before I pull her lips toward me.

But Asura doesn't seem to like the slow pace I'm going.

She tangles her hands into my hair and pulls my lips harshly into hers. It confirms, in a way, that

97

she wants me as much as I want her. I close my eyes, enjoying the sweetness of her full, soft lips again. Our lips move together as I run a hand over her hips and pull her flush against my body.

She gasps slightly, letting me slip my tongue right into her mouth. She doesn't pull back. Instead, she swirls her tongue around mine, fighting for dominance. Her lust and desire sweeten the air. I pull back to kiss along her jaw before getting to her ear. "Look who wants who more."

She grips my shoulder, tilting her head so I can kiss up and down her neck. Her pulse quickens under my lips. "Shut up," she hisses between moans.

I would give anything to hear her cry, beg, and moan again. My arms wrap around her waist, one is running up her spine.

She pulls back to take my lips against hers again.

I pull back as I hear someone below us open the door and climb the stairs. I move a bit from her body to ensure it doesn't seem like the heir is kissing me. She bites her lip, saying good night to us as they pass us.

"Good night," I answer, voice drunk on lust.

She bursts into laughter as soon as she hears the door open and close above us. "Uh... I guess that's the cue for me to go. I have school tomorrow."

"Oh, weird. Me too," I tease.

Asura smiles at me, and I return it. *Her smile is too fucking pretty...* I push her silver hair back and pull her lips back to mine for a moment. "Good night, princess."

She licks her lips, probably still tasting mine. "Good night, Ledge." She moves up the stairs, and I watch for a moment before turning to go back down. "Ledge, your jacket!" I almost hear her start back down the steps.

"Keep it, baby girl," I shout and close the stairwell door behind me. She already has a nickname for me, but then again, she has one for everyone. I'm not special; I am just a low-level demon that happens to be a hellhound guardian. *I wish I had met her sooner. She could have been my Soul Reaper, obviously having a better point of view of us as hellhounds than Khazon does.*

## Asura

*The sound of falling rock fills the air, and it makes me turn to the noise. Behind me, my home, the palace of Hell, is burning. The flames are hotter than any flame in Hell has ever been. My eyes burn with tears as I watch every brick fall against the ground, tumbling into the canyon below.*

*I turn to see Hell. In the distance, I watch as Lucifer's castle breaks apart in the same fashion, making me sob, "How do I fix this?"*

## Hell's Reaper

*"The war is coming faster than you think,"* my own voice says to myself.

War? Is this still the future for my home? Death and destruction? I left Hell with the vision of this happening if I took the throne. Hell will fall under my reign.

*But then, the day before Khazon came for me, I had the same dream but watched it as it fell under Derrick's reign.*

No matter what... Hell will fall.

My eyes flutter open, staring at the ceiling from my bed. My dad said heirs always have visions, sometimes in the form of dreams. He said they will always come true, and we must deal with the aftermath. When I asked if he had ever been able to change a vision, he simply shook his head.

Sitting up, I glance at my phone, seeing it's almost time to get up. I roll out of bed and decide to shower. Going to the bathroom, I see Ledger's jacket on the sink, and *I wonder if he's up*...He did give me his number yesterday before the restaurant, but how desperate will I look if I text him? Closing my eyes, I see that reaper's blood-spattered face and how Ledger would have killed him for touching me. All night, I have been replaying us having sex over and over in my head.

I open my phone, biting my lip. Just as I send the good morning text, his icon pops up, and starts typing. *He's up.* I set my phone down, waiting impatiently for the phone to go off.

The heir, *me,* isn't known for dating anyone. Even in Earthbound, I didn't care to date any humans.

My phone dings just as the water in the shower starts getting hot.

**Ledge**: How many times did you orgasm to me last night?

I snort.

**Me**: Too many times to count. You?

It wasn't exactly a lie.

**Ledge**: I lost count too… Good morning, though. Didn't actually think you'd text me.

**Me**: I almost thought about blocking you, but I think you can be useful to have around.

I set the phone down to get ready for the day. I take my time showering before I get out to text Ledger and get dressed. I didn't feel like wearing a skirt, so I opted for the ugly black khaki pants. I roll them up at the bottom, just above my boots. I put on my button-down and then Ledger's windbreaker jacket. I let my silver curly hair do whatever it wants, leaving it down for now. I grab my bag before moving out of the dorm room.

**Ledge**: Breakfast?

**Me**: Read my mind. Going now.

I don't beat the hellhound to breakfast, but I find him with a group. Our eyes meet, and he nods to the seat next to him, which is open. I bite my lip and grab food before moving to their table and confidently sit next to Ledger, who shifts for me to have enough space.

"You said no one can sit next to you!" one of the hellhounds whines across the table, slamming down his fork.

"Yeah, and?" Ledger grumbles, making me look up at him. *Fucker moved his friends for me?*

"Rude... I thought we had something!" he teases.

Ledger lets out a sigh. "Hazen, Benson, and Gibby, meet Asura."

The guy who was whining leans in. That is Hazen. His silver-blue eyes wander up and down me. "Oh, I see why you're all giddy today."

Ledger grumbles something, eating his food.

I lock eyes with Hazen. I can lie and say Hazen is ugly, but he's not. His hair is cut, similar to Ledger's, with the sides shaved, but Hazen has a curly mohawk hanging down from the top and back. His golden tan skin compliments his gray eyes. He has a few piercings, one in his nose, three spikes at the top of each of his ears and plugs through his stretched ears. His body is just as huge and wide as Ledgers and the other hellhounds.

Hazen holds out his hand. "Nice to you, Heir."

I take his hand, glancing down as his magic shocks me but not enough to make me pull away. "Electric or lightning hound?" I question.

"Technically, both," he says with a smirk, flashing his canine teeth.

*Oh, bite me, please.* I clamp my thighs shut.

"As you can see," Ledger says, making me pry my eyes from Hazen. "Hazen is desperate."

The hound named Gibby snorts. "For *pussy*."

"For a Soul Reaper," Ledger finishes, growling passively.

I nod. *Lucky for me.* I catch a look at one of the hounds walking by; He looks the same as he did yesterday. He rolls his lime-green eyes and keeps walking to his spot in the corner. "And Jigsaw?" I question out loud.

Hazen lets out a chuckle. "Saw wants to be on no one's team, but he and I are actually good friends."

I turn back, cocking a brow.

He touches his heart through his jacket. "I don't lie." His eyes fall on my jacket. "Hey, isn't that—"

Amos cuts in at the right time. "Move over, mountains." Hazen moves over a seat, laughing, and now Amos is sitting across from me.

"Who said you can sit with us?" Ledger teases.

She sends him a glare. "She was my friend first. You can move, lover boy."

Ledger lets out a chuckle, hand brushing my hip. "Whatever, Grim."

I snort, shaking my head. "We are off-topic." I lean over to Hazen, across Ledger a bit to get close enough, and I can tell by the hard-on he sports that he doesn't care. "Talk to Saw for me?"

Hazen nods.

Ledger let out a noise. "Really, him, though? He's…"

103

"Toxic," Gibby says.

"Asshole," Benson adds.

"Hot," Amos concludes, making me smile.

*Ledger makes another noise.*

I lean into him and whisper, "Your jealousy is showing."

He growls. *Will Ledger beat up Jigsaw if he becomes my hound?*

Hazen snorts. "That's why he punched that ice hound."

"Shut it," Ledger snaps. He grows warm against my side.

I let out a laugh. "So, it wasn't because he was an asshole, huh?"

"He is, though," he says, looking away. He's probably regretting letting me sit with his friends, but we seem to have a lot of fun teasing and joking around.

I see Killian at one point and wave at him, and he waves back, trying to hide the hickey on his neck with his collar.

"Who would have thought the Princess of Hell is so close to her brother? Aren't siblings supposed to hate each other like Miya and me?" Amos teases.

I snort. "But my brothers are so precious! We just grew up close," I say with a shrug. "Plus, they are not as fucking annoying as Miya."

"Someone's jealous," Gibby mutters.

"Of what?" I question, looking up and sipping my drink.

"He's implying you are jealous she's with Khazon," Ledger deadpans.

I throw my head back. *"Or?* I'm pissed she called me trash the first time I met her. I don't care who Khaz is dating; She's probably just as annoying without him."

Hazen nods. "She is."

I shake my head, giggling. "I don't get jealous; It's not a trait I have."

"So, if a girl came up to Ledger, kissed him, and implied they should fuck, you wouldn't be pissed?" Hazen asks.

I lean forward, eyes moving up and down him. "I'd ask to watch."

Hazen's brow bounces.

Khazon walks in with Miya and two other Soul Reapers with him. His jaw clenches when he sees who we are all sitting with. I wave with a smile, earning an eye roll. He moves to us. "Please tell me my hellhound has no involvement over Jake getting the shit kicked out of him?"

*Jake. That is who Ledger beat up yesterday?*

Amos meets my eyes, a questioning look filling them. I haven't told her everything yet.

"Who?" I tilt my head.

"I'm not stupid, Asura."

I hold up my hands. "I never said you were, Khazzie; I just asked a question. We only went out for sushi yesterday."

"I wasn't invited," Hazen says with a huff.

105

"You said you were busy," Ledger grumbles.

"Never for sushi." Hazen pouts, sitting back. I watch as his strong arms cross over his chest.

"Asura, if I found out that you involved my hound with this, I'll—"

My eyes snap to him, feeling pressured. "You'll do what? What can you, the Son of Death, do to the Heir of Hell?"

He straightens, and I take in his looks for a moment. He is in a red uniform like mine. His hair is getting a bit shaggy and long, but he is very handsome with his dark features. His eyes are hard and on me. "Jake is my friend."

"Is he okay?"

He nods.

"Next time, tell him to keep his hands to himself, and I won't have to fuck him up."

His eyes scan my face as he lets out a breath. I can tell he's trying to process everything, and he seems to believe it because he walks away. Ledger and I break off from his friends when breakfast is made as we walk with Amos to my class.

"Why would you cover for me?" Ledger asks, grabbing my shoulder to stop. I look up at him. He's looking good in his black button-up and black khaki pants; I just know his butt looks amazing in them.

"Where is your class at?" I question, distracting him.

He sends me a look. "Asura."

"Ledger." I lift my chin slightly. Silence thickens between us.

"God…" Amos buts in. "You guys just need to fuck already."

My tongue flicks out across my lips as I smirk up at Ledger. Slowly, the corners of his mouth curl.

"No fucking way, and you didn't tell me?!" Amos grabs me, making me draw my attention to her.

I chuckle. "I'll tell you about it later, weirdo."

She scoffs, touching my shoulder. "Oh. Where did you get this jacket from? It's cute," Amos teases as we start walking again. The jacket obviously belongs to a hound, and it's basically a dress on my body.

I smirk. "Oh, you know, from a dog."

Ledger makes a noise somewhere between a laugh and a snort. At the classroom door, he leans down and whispers in my ear, "I'll see you later, *princess.*" Heat rushes through my body before he moves away. He glances back over his shoulder at me. I lick my lips, wanting to taste him again.

"Tell me about it!" Amos says, pushing me and breaking me from my trance.

I roll my eyes, following Amos into class. "He beat the shit out of that guy, and we just… had sex against a building."

Amos closes her eyes with a soft moan. "Why are you living my fucking dream? Was he bloody?"

I hum in confirmation.

She grasps, making a whining noise. "Lucky bitch."

## Hell's Reaper

Khazon and Miya sit before us in their regular seats in the first class we had together. He glares at me the whole class.

I wonder what's got him so pissed.

# Asura

*Thud!*

Inarian throws me over his shoulder and onto the mat below.

A gasp escapes my throat as my eyes close. Everything aches. Between this and the weapons training, I'm sore. Inarian doesn't show any mercy, but I'm learning a lot about fighting and his fighting style. If I keep training like this, it might help me, but I know right now that my back will have a huge bruise.

"Are you all right?" Inarian finally asks, kneeling next to me.

I open my eyes, taking in each vibration of his rich voice. He rarely talks, didn't yesterday. Hazen said that he would likely not speak to anyone at all, only a few words at a time. I take a shaky breath. "Oh…Peachy."

He let out a sigh. "Did I hurt you again?"

I roll my eyes before rolling onto my hands and knees to get up. "Stop treating me like I'm weak; I'm anything but weak. Again."

He cocks a brow.

"Again!" I say sternly.

With a sigh, he rushes at me, and I prepare for it. His fist swings and I dodge with my forearm. I wince; *That'll hurt later.* Instead of punching, I jump up and kick him in the chest.

Inarian barely moves, reaching for my ankle.

Scrambling, I drop quickly, dodging his next punches. I swing my leg, and it makes him fall hard against the mat.

*Thud!*

Quickly, I take advantage of this and climb onto him, straddling his hips. My fist flies, but of course, he's fast, grabbing my wrists. He lifts his hips, taking control and flipping us. I struggle against him as he pins my hands to the mat below me.

Our crotches line up, making me freeze. An icy chill run through me, making me shudder below him. His dark eyes glance down at where our body is connected.

"What? Are you going to get turned on by every guy who pins you down? What if I was an enemy?"

I can't help but chuckle. "I'd probably be turned on more. Danger is fun."

He rolls his eyes, shifting to get up.

"How could you tell?" I roll onto all fours and bounce to my feet.

He cocks a brow, fixing his shirt.

"That... I'm turned on," I whisper.

"As hellhounds, we have heightened senses. Like how your heart raced and your... smell changed."

My face heats up. "Everyone can tell?" He nods. "Oh god!"

He shrugs. "It happens." He fixes his shirt, and I can see the faint outline of his dick through the gray sweats. *I turned him on... Does this happen with each girl that smells or something? Hazen said he didn't have many girls in and out of his life when I asked if Inarian was single. He doesn't even have a reaper.*

"Hey, you don't have a Soul Reaper, right?"

He doesn't answer me. Instead, he glares down at me with an icy gaze. I can tell he's trying to intimidate me, but compared to my father, this was nothing.

"You should be my hound."

"No," he deadpans, turning and moving to the water fountain.

I race after him. "What do you mean, *no*?"

"Are you not used to that word?" Inarian asks.

"I know what it means, ass. I'm just curious why."

He grumbles something, leaning to drink from the water fountain, but when he pushes the button, the whole water fountain, including the water coming out of it, freezes. He groans and pulls away. Quickly, it thaws and turns back to liquid.

I move beside it, pushing the button. I feel his icy eyes on me, and I wait until he stands up and is done to stop pushing the button. "Does that always happen?"

He lets out a huff. "Only when I'm pissed."

I smirk, looking up at him. "Are my questions pissing you off?"

He glares at me. "Yes."

"So just agree to be my hound."

He laughs a harsh deep chuckle. "When you can barely take me down or hold your own? You're weak, and I would never be caught dead protecting someone like *you*."

The bell rings at the perfect time, letting him walk out of the gym.

His words stung. I never considered myself weak. But, in this form, maybe I am. I was no match for Draco and his men or any hellhound here. I am at a lower level, while all my friends are above me. *Khazon got stronger... Can I?*

"Don't take it to heart," Amos says, touching my back. "He had a Soul Reaper but failed to protect her."

I look at her, watching her leave me behind. *Is he scared that he is going to fail again?* "If he's not looking for a reaper, why else is he here?"

She shrugs. "Heard it's for money."

Before I can ask more, I feel heat behind me. "Are you okay?" Ledger's voice comes from behind me.

I nod. "Leave him alone today; I pissed him off."

The fire hellhound cocks a brow. "Why do you care?"

I glance up at him. "You know, for the future Queen of Hell, I'm actually a nice person sometimes."

A smirk runs across his lips. "I guess."

I scoff, punching him.


"Getting hellhounds is proving harder than I thought," I say to Amos as we are in line for lunch.

She snorts. "That's because you're stubborn and go after the ones that don't fucking want you."

I laugh with her. "Rude. Everyone wants me." I turn around to sit down just as my tray is hit out of my hands by flying hands. It clatters to the floor, and the room seemingly becomes silent. I look down at the wasted food I just paid for and then up at Miya. Every day feels like there is something new happening, especially with her.

She stares at me.

"That was rude, don't you think?" I huff.

113

She laughs, stepping over the food and into my face. "Whore." She shoves her phone in my face, where there's a picture of Ledger and me kissing in the stairwell.

I grit my teeth into a smile. They don't need to know it bothers me. "Send me that; It's hot."

"And this?" she says, swiping her thumb to the side.

The next is a video of me dancing on Ledger at the club the night he found me. It's from a side angle. That one made me smile. "Damn, I look good. Send that to me too."

She scoffs. "Do you like pissing off Khazon? He's mine, you know."

I throw my head back and laugh. "Please, I don't want him. You have proof that I'm focused on someone else, yet *you* are very insecure in your relationship."

"I just know women, and I know what you are really after," she says, stepping close. "Bitches like you are crazy."

My eyes snap to her. *Show her crazy...* the voice in my head says.

My tongue flicks over my lips. I glance over as the cafeteria doors open, and my eyes lock with Khazon's. "Guess who had him first..." I whisper.

Miya gasps, and her ivory face turns bright red. "You... you fucking whore!" Magic swirls in the air, tickling against my skin, making me laugh. Compared to me in this form, she's weaker and knows it. She

114

might have struck me if she thought she was stronger than me. "Come on, A," I say, circling her. "Oh, Miya." I turn back to the fuming girl. "Send me that picture and the video, please." I walk away with my back turned. She's not going to attack with my back to her. I have no issue with protecting myself, especially from someone like her.

Khazon grabs my arms just as I'm about to leave. "What the fuck did you do to her?"

I cock a brow, ripping my arm from his grasp. "Ask your little girlfriend, Khaz."

## Khazon

My blood is boiling, and I don't understand why everyone is either laughing or staring at Miya. Ledger meets my eyes, but he makes me just as *mad*. I glance down at my phone to see Ledger and Asura swapping spit with each other. Miya sent it to me, saying she doesn't want Ledger to get distracted. I know she's lying, but I appreciate it.

I move to my girl. "Are you okay?"

Miya's face is extremely red, and her magic barely licks my skin. She's so much weaker compared to the others. I told her that if she focused a bit more on her powers, she would succeed as a Soul Reaper. But Miya is focused on being the prettiest in the school, how she dresses, or how her hair falls. "She's so annoying. She thinks she's hot shit because she's the devil's daughter. Big deal. The devil has a whore for a daughter."

My eyes snap to her, and she quickly closes her mouth.

Asura is anything but a whore, no matter what she does or who she does. I don't even like that word and have told Miya, but it seems to be stuck in her limited vocabulary.

Slowly, I pry my eyes from her to look at my hounds and jerk my chin. *They know what I mean.* Every eye in the mess hall is locked on us, and I step over the food. "Nothing to see here."

No one moves.

"Fuck off!" I bark loudly. Finally, they all go back to talking, but I know it's going to be about Asura. She's been the non-stop talk since arriving. Now she's fucking with my hounds, and I don't like that.

As soon as we get to their dorms, I start questioning them. "Who took that video at the strip club?"

Ledger raises a brow, sitting back on the couch. "What video?"

I know he didn't take it; It wasn't taken from his angle. I already knew it was Andrew, but I wanted to hear it from him.

"It was me; I thought it was..." Andrew starts, looking down.

"Hot? Something you could masturbate to later, huh?" I finish, looking at Ledger. "He took a video of Asura giving you a lap dance."

He cocks a brow. "Mhm. Okay... Now everyone has seen it?"

I nod.

"Shit."

"And now there's a photo of you two kissing in the Soul Reaper's stairwell."

He holds my gaze. "And?" *He doesn't care.*

"Stay away from her," I order.

"Excuse me?" he almost growls.

"Stay *the fuck* away from her," I repeat myself.

"*Why?*"

I glare at him. "I'm your reaper, and if you want to keep me as your reaper—so you don't get *fucking* kicked out—then I suggest you do what I say. If I see one more thing about you two talking or walking each other to class like you have a fucking schoolgirl crush, you'll be gone. And I know this is your last offense, Ledger."

He glares at me in disbelief, but he also knows I will do it. I'm serious about my group. "Is it because you fucked her?"

I scoff. "Excuse me?" Inside, my stomach drops.

"You fucked her, didn't you?"

I snort. "Like I'd ever—"

"She told Miya that she had you first."

I try to read his body language, but I can't. *Why would she tell Miya that after attacking Miya?* Miya said that Asura knocked her food out of her hands and told her to stay away from me… I guess it makes sense to say that to piss Miya off. "Fuck off! I'd never fuck someone like her. We were just childhood friends, nothing more, nothing less. Now we are nothing. No one goes near Asura or talks to her."

"Except for you," Ledger says.

I glare at him, and he glares back. "I won't be talking to her after this, and I promise that." Asura has already stirred the pot too much, creating drama between my hounds and me, fighting reapers, and trying to fight my girlfriend.

# Asura

"You've been here for three days and are already starting drama." Amos giggles the next day.

Honestly, it'd be funny if I was in a better mood. Ledger didn't talk to me at all, and he didn't even look at me at dinner. I wasn't one to beg, so I stopped trying. I get on my knees for no man, and I certainly don't beg for attention from anyone.

In line at the mess hall, I glance over to see Khazon, and his little girlfriend walk in hand-in-hand. His hounds follow like puppy dogs. I know Khazon had something to do with all of this; He tried to get me to stay away from Ledger in the first place.

My eyes meet Ledger's bright red eyes. I shouldn't blame him or be pissed at him; It's not his fault he has a shitty Soul Reaper. I was more pissed that I had just met this guy and started *liking* him.

Don't get me wrong.

Ledger makes me laugh harder than most guys have, and he always has witty replies to mine. He and I have talked about anything we like, from music to food. And he's a hellfire hellhound with a sexy ass body... *Where was I going with this? Oh yeah.* But I met him last week. I do not get attached to men easily, but something about these men is making me lose my damn mind. I've never felt so secure and safe around anyone before.

I turn around, bumping into someone, and, instead of slapping my tray down like Miya, they catch it.

"Watch it before there's a repeat of yesterday," a heavy rough voice says.

I look and lock eyes with Jigsaw, the toxic hellhound. I glance down to see his gloved hand steadying my tray. "Are you sure you don't want to just... hit it out of my hand and call me a whore?"

I can tell he smiles under the leather mask by the way his lime-green eyes push up at the corner. "Now, why would I do that? All the hounds know you were turned on by being called a whore."

My jaw drops as he walks away. My eyes travel down to his jeans with chains on them. When I look back up, our eyes meet. *He watched me look at his ass.*

"See, you are already moving on," Amos says.

"It's different." I want both Jigsaw and Ledger at once, and Hazen could even join in.

Amos grabs my hand just as I enter the reaper dorm house after Thursday night dinner. "There's a Halloween party tonight," she says.

I look up. "On a Thursday night?"

"We don't have classes tomorrow because of the telum ceremony," she says, jumping around. "Let's forget men and go drink in the Shadow World and have fun!"

I smirk. "You had me at Halloween party."

Amos squeals, almost jumping with joy.

"But I don't have a costume for it," I say. I wonder if this is really a good idea. It is the day before the ceremony where we get our weapons for soul reaping, and all Amos is thinking about is getting drunk.

"I have a costume for you." She smiles wickedly. We spent the next hour and a half preparing for the costume party. Even though I hadn't been here for long, I almost forgot that it was fall. There are no seasons in the Shadow World, just dull-everlasting warm weather. The outfit Amos gave me should be classified as lingerie. The top is lace, barely covering my pierced nipples, and has a little skirt to cover my white thong. A halo sits around my head. Amos wears the same type of clothing, but red, with two red horns on her head.

Amos and I step out of the taxi that we ordered. I can hear the music blaring from down the street from the house. Mansion, really. I wasn't even sure who lived here or who was throwing the party. The house is almost as large as the palace. Apparently, they have these types of parties all the time, especially right before and after ceremonies.

"Who will all be here?" I ask as if I know anyone.

"Most people from the academy. Nothing too crazy," she says.

*Crazy* seems to explain what is going on inside thoroughly. People dance in the massive living room, with speakers shaking the room more than the stomping. People are drinking and making out in the hall. I pass someone who blows smoke at me, and I roll my eyes, moving on. Amos gets pulled by someone toward the very lovely matte black kitchen, and like a puppy, I follow. I don't know many people here, despite them all knowing who I am.

Amos bumps into Miya just as we make it to the kitchen.

Her blue eyes find me, and she makes a noise. "Look at what the trash brought in."

"You and this obsession with trash…" I chuckle, moving away from her, but she steps in my way.

"Are you always dressed like a slut?" she shoots at me, earning laughter from her little group of girls. "Is it because you are one?"

I smile sweetly. "Does it get you off to put women down for what they want to do?"

122

She rolls her eyes. "I like to call it how I see it. Like"—her eyes travel behind me to someone over my shoulder—"how you throw yourself at multiple guys at once. We all know why you are really here."

*To stop a war and claim my throne? To figure out my father's cryptic message? So, I can find hellhounds that are loyal to me?*

"To get new clients for your stripping. To sleep with as many guys as possible and to break up Ledger and Khazon."

I roll my eyes. "Is it only me you're calling a whore? Do you feel threatened that I am comfortable with my sexuality and body? Stripping sucked. I met a million people like you, but I was in control. You can call me a slut until you are blue in the face, but you will never make me feel bad for doing what I want with my body."

She glances around at the small crowd that surrounds us. "All you think about is who to fuck next. The hounds said you're always hor—"

"Fucking is fun. Sorry if Khazon brings you no pleasure," I say with a snort.

Her face turns a blazing red, and I see her demon surfacing.

Khazon appears behind her. "Is there a problem here?"

I tilt my head, looking up at him. "Nope." I twist around, locking eyes with Ledger, who towers over me.

## Hell's Reaper

How come when guys are hypersexual, they aren't called sluts or whores? Men applaud them for fucking as many women as they can. I think about having sex with a few different guys, and suddenly, I'm the whore. Those words alone—slut or whore—are degrading, and the next person who mutters it will face my demon.

Moving away from them, I grab some juice the party hosts have made with fruit and alcohol. Amos does the same, catching up with someone else. I lean against the counter, looking out into the living room. The house looks massive and belongs to someone rich, but with all the people in the place, it makes it feel smaller. The living room has been turned into a dance floor with a speaker playing on the floor loudly. I feel eyes burning into me, making me glance around.

Ledger's hard red eyes are still on me, but he has moved away from where we were.

Finally, I take in his features, letting my dark eyes roam his body and study his dark hair falling against his forehead. Red horns are on his head, and he's wearing a red T-shirt and jeans with combat boots. His costume is so subtle, yet he makes it look so sexy. I reach up and touch the halo.

He smirks behind his beer glass. I can tell by the way his eyes sparkle and the creases under his eyes move. *Fuck... I want to see his smile and hear his voice tell me a stupid joke.*

Khazon bumps into him. His lips move, and the smile from Ledger disappears.

I roll my eyes.

"You think he told Ledger to stay away?" Amos questions, turning her attention back to me.

"For sure. Khazon seems extremely jealous, and I'm unsure why."

"He definitely wants you."

I gag, wishing Ledger would just watch me again. Look at me, wanting attention from a man. "I'm going to dance, and Ledger will have to look at this ass shaking."

Amos chokes on her drink. "Asura! You naughty angel."

I grab her hand, swaying my hips, as I pull her to the dance floor, rounding the sea of people. I'm a flirt when it comes to dancing, which was worse in the club. I know how to roll my hips to draw attention to me. I know how to move my body to give all the men boners. But I don't care about everyone else. I care about drawing Ledger's attention; *I want his attention.*

Amos dances with me. She moves just as seductively as I do, but her eyes dart to Ledger every few minutes.

Suddenly, I didn't care about anyone else as the alcohol I chugged tingled under my skin. I missed this. I miss dancing, and I miss losing myself in the music. My hand comes up my chest and runs up my throat. I close my eyes, losing myself in the music. I dance like I would in a regular dancing club, like when I used to go with my human friends. They always said that I would draw all the attention to myself. I didn't pay any mind half of the time, having too much fun to stop dancing.

Dancing has become a stress reliever. Earth had a lot of stressors; between money and work, I wasn't always good at saving. I used to drink a lot and tried different types of Earthly drugs. None of them were ever as strong as the drugs in the Shadow World, but they always did the trick. On top of that, I was homesick and never thought I'd ever be able to return.

Amos touches my hand, drawing me back to reality. "Damn girl, I'm drooling."

I throw my head back, giggling.

"He's watching," she mutters.

I do a spin, pushing my hips out a bit to add it to my dancing. Ledger's eyes are hard on me, making me smirk. Then I see Khazon's dark eyes on me with his jaw tight.

"I feel like throwing one-dollar bills at you," she teases as I turn my attention back to her.

"Men are so easy to get attention from. Shake your ass, and they drool."

"Not for me," she says, but she doesn't seem mad. Some girls, like Miya, seem to strive for all men's attention, then ruin the women that have it. Example: me. I don't want all the guys' attention. I want Ledger's… and maybe Inarian's and Jigsaw's, but neither are here. *They don't seem like the party type.*

Electricity makes me jolt, and I feel hands grabbing my hips. "Just me," a familiar voice whispers in my ear, but I can't fully determine who. I shudder. "I see that we are pissing off Ledger."

I snort, turning and looking up. *It's Hazen;* His curls are loosely done with bright green hair chalk rubbed through it. His golden-tan skin is covered with a bit of white makeup and a giant red smile. *The Joker.* "Not pissing him off; we're getting his attention."

"You got a lot of people's attention... Mine included. Can I dance with you?"

"Can you even dance?" I tease.

He grabs my hand, spinning me so my back is to him before pressing his crotch right into my ass as he follows my hips with the beat. I widen my eyes, feeling my head spin. He moves just as well as I do. "Can *I* dance?" His warm breath is on my neck, making me hot.

I turn my head, letting his hands guide my hips. "Don't you dare turn me on, not with all these hounds."

He chuckles heavily in my ear. "Try not to get turned on." His ringed fingers run up my stomach slightly, making me stiffen. "Do *you* even know how to dance?"

*Two can play at that game.* I scoff, ducking around his arm and circling him. My hands run up his chest, over his shoulder, down to his back. He's tall like the other hounds, maybe the shortest at seven feet. "Don't insult me. I'm sure you saw the video."

He shakes his head, pulling me against his chest. "I don't feed into rumors or listen to them." I look up at him. He's wearing a suit that barely hides any of his muscles.

"Joker? How toxic," I comment.

He snorts, "Me? Toxic? At least I'm not trying to make hounds jealous."

I glance at Ledger, whose jaw is tight and his grip around his beer is harsh.

"Your little boyfriend told him not to go around you, or he wouldn't be his reaper anymore."

*Boyfriend? Khazon?* "That motherfucker," I mutter.

"He is so mad that I'm dancing with you."

I glance at Khazon and see his chest rising and falling hard. Smirking, I turn, putting my ass against his hard dick, and together we move so perfectly. He guides me a bit until I take over. Suddenly, this isn't about pissing Khazon off; I realize how large Hazen is against me. Heat fills me.

Hazen presses his lips into my ear. "You smell good enough to eat."

My eyes close, and I can almost imagine this alternative punk guy right between my legs giving me what I'm begging for. Then he would sink his canine teeth right into my thigh, taking my breath away at the thought and causing me to push from him.

"I need to go to the bathroom. Sorry!" I move through the kitchen and down the hall. I don't even know where the bathroom is, but I'm determined to find it. Once I do, I close the door behind me and fan myself. *Men need to stop being so... hot. Before I lose my mind and fuck them all.* I move to the sink, running my hands under the cold water. I barely know Ledger or Hazen, and the desire for them both is the strongest feeling I've ever felt before.

The bathroom door opens, making me whip around. "Occupied!" I say quickly. I half expected it to be Hazen for more, but Ledger stands staring hard at me instead.

# Asura

The room gets ten times hotter as Ledger reaches behind him and locks the door.

"Ledge?" I turn off the sink behind me; He doesn't say anything. Ledger *did* just beat up a stranger for touching me, and imagine what he's going to do to Hazen, his best friend. Dancing with Hazen made me forget all about how Ledger and I had sex. And about the stranger he almost killed.

He sets down his beer on the shelf before moving to me. I back up the closer he gets, nerves running through me. I doubt Ledger would do anything to hurt me, but he grasps my throat harshly and then slams his lips into mine.

A gasp escapes my throat, and I have to blink away my confusion. *Why would he kiss me? Is it to*

130

*claim me? Fuck it.* Lust and heat run through me as I kiss him back instantly, fisting his shirt. He pushes me into the counter, my back stinging from the pain. I groan, but he lifts me and puts me on the counter, grinding his stiff cock into my core. A moan slips passed my lips.

He pulls back. "You're mine," he growls, heat from his skin kissing mine.

I grip his hair and pull. "I'm no ones. You don't like Hazen's cock on me? You don't like him touching me?"

He looks down at me, jaw-tightening. "No."

"Too damn bad. You're going to have to suffer and watch him touch me and turn me on," I say with a smirk, guiding his lips back to mine.

He growls.

But I tighten my fist in his hair, chuckling. "Bad boy," I tease.

He grabs my hips and pulls me flush against him. Our cores line up, and suddenly I'm reminded of how big he is. I roll my hips right against his cock. "You want me, right?" he teases.

I swallow hard. "No."

"Just admit you want me, and I will give you what you want."

My eyes widen. "Ledger."

He fists my hair, making me arch my back and look up at him. "I'll take you right here, right now. Say it."

I lick my lips. "Make me."

Hell's Reaper

A smirk runs on his lips as he drops to his knees. Even on his knees, he still looks taller than me. His hands run up my outer thighs and lift the small white skirt I have on. His fingers knead the sore flesh on my thighs, and even though they are already spread, my legs open further. Then he freezes before his crimson eyes lock with me as he leans forward. His lips curl as he softly kisses my skin.

My eyes close. *What I would give to be eaten right now.*

His teeth sink into my flesh, and I cry out. Laughter rumbles in his throat. "Say it."

Between him and Hazen, my panties are soaked, and I feel the juice dripping down my thighs. He sinks his teeth into my skin harder when I don't say it. My hips buck, but my teeth bite my lips to stop the noise.

Ledger's eyes lock onto my panty-covered core. "God... You're so wet. Do you want me to please you?"

I swallow, looking down at him.

Finally, he reaches forward and traces where my clit is. A deep ache runs through me. I want him more than I'd like to admit. His cock felt so good pounding into me the first time, and I can only imagine what his mouth would feel like. "Tell me what you need, princess."

And when the pad of his fingers brushes my pulsing clit, I throw my head back. "You. I need you. Please."

132

He makes a noise of satisfaction before finally pushing my white panties to the side and running his long, rough tongue through my soaked folds.

I let out a sigh, head dropping back.

"Mhm," he mutters, pulling my hips closer to the edge of the sink counter. "You taste so fucking good, baby." That's when he devours me, tasting me like a crazed, hungry man. He does it with such skill I've never had before. My thighs shake as I push my heels into the thick muscles of his back.

"Fuck, Ledger."

He hums, tongue flicking my clit. My legs shake to the pace of the constant flickering.

My eyes roll back, and my hips begin to buck. My breathing is getting heavier than it's ever been. I can't believe this is going to be quick.

Ledger pulls back. "Fuck, he's coming."

*He?* "I'm coming!" I try to push his mouth back to me. It was *right* there. The tingling in my limbs has already started.

His eyes snap to me. "Oh? The Princess of Hell wants to come? Mhm… Beg."

A gasp escapes my lips. "Ledger, don't do this."

"Whose pussy is this?"

I lick my dry lips. "Yours."

"So, beg."

I punch the counter as a flash of rage rushes through me. "Fuck! No!"

Ledger's long tongue circles his mouth. "I'm leaving. Come out in like ten minutes. Calm yourself down." His eyes drop to my shaking legs. His veiny hands fix his crotch until you can barely see his cock. It should be illegal to conceal something that massive in your pants and have no one know. He leans down, taking my lips with his.

The smell and taste of my pussy overwhelm me, causing me to close my thighs tightly.

*I want to stop him from leaving... But what would I look like? The Heir of Hell begging for dick.*

"Bye, Princess."

I let out a soft sigh. "Goodbye, Hound."

He smirks, leaving the bathroom quickly. I take the next few minutes cleaning and fixing my clothes; If Hazen dances on me like that again, I might burst all over him. I leave the bathroom, bumping into a large frame. Gasping, I look up.

Khazon glares down at me.

"What's your problem now, Angel of Death?"

"Was Ledger in there with you?" he growls.

I snort at the tone of his voice. He's trying to intimidate me. "Yeah, he held my clit up while I pissed. *No*, remember you told him to stay away from me, or you'd make him leave your reaper group."

Khazon's face pales.

"Oh, yeah, I know about that," I say. "Hazen told me."

"Listen, it's not—" he starts.

"If you think you can control me and my life, you are sadly mistaken. No man will ever have any type of control over me."

He looks at me like I hurt him. He lets out a huff, running a head through his hair. "You don't understand. Ledger isn't a good guy, he fucks women, and he moves on; It won't last."

I roll my eyes. "Who said we wanted to date or anything? If it's just a hookup to him, then it is to me too."

But I didn't believe that. I doubt Ledger can stay away from me, and maybe we'd be friends with benefits. I've never been one to settle down, either. Speechless, I leave him in the hall. Grabbing another drink from the kitchen, I search for Amos.

An unfamiliar hand touches my hip, making me spin fast.

My eyes meet with a purple gaze. "Hello," he says, moving close. *Incubus.* His magic flicks and licks my skin, giving me goosebumps, but I don't feel the lust he wants me to feel. "I'm Nathan."

*Now the real question is, how bored am I to feed into this?* "Hello. Asura."

He takes my hand, kissing the top of it. His magic lingers against my skin as lust fills his purple eyes. "Do you want to get out of here?"

I try not to laugh in his face. *You have to be really confident in your magic to instantly think someone is going to go home with you that quickly, especially the Heir of Hell.*

The laugh comes from someone else. "Oh, Nathan, didn't anyone tell you that the Princess of Hell is immune to your bullshit?"

I look up and lock eyes with someone who looks familiar. His pitch-black eyes lock on mine, and a smirk curls at the side of his lips. His black hair hangs past his shoulders, almost to his hips.

"Shut it, Ozias," Nathan says. "I'm about to get her to go home with me." He touches my arm again, but I can easily move away even though he's strong and his magic is there. "Ozzy?"

He raises a brow. "You remember me now, Heir?"

"Oh, shut up!" I move to him, wrapping my arms around his body, and he does the same, running a hand to my waist to pull back. "How are your parents?" *Hades and Persephone made a handsome ass son.*

"Good," he says, looking down at me. He's a year older than me, but I have always been taller than him. Seems like he had a growth spurt since I've been gone, and he's gotten hotter too. "You should go and see them; they miss you."

"Hey, Asura, let's get out of here," Nathan says, making me realize he's still here.

Ozias begins laughing so hard I think he is going to piss himself, then he deadpans, "Go the fuck away, Nathan."

The incubus scurries away.

I look up at him, hitting his arm. "Why are you so rude?"

"You can't tell me that you thought he was cute!" Ozias leans against the counter. He's dressed like a priest with everything black, but nothing about Ozzy has ever been holy. Dirty thoughts run through my head. I wouldn't mind getting on my knees and worshiping him. He's towering over me now, and I can tell he works out, but he's not as big as Khazon.

I roll my eyes, leaning against the counter. "I thought I was getting lucky tonight."

Ozzy stands up straight but leans toward me. "You still can. Lots of men saw you dancing."

"Oh... you saw that?" *Is he flirting? With me?* We grew up together. I never looked at him like that, but he seemed more grown up and way more handsome than before. His features are thin, besides his square jaw, and his skin lacks any color. He could definitely pass as a vampire. His hair is way longer than it's ever been, and his black eyes have this icy glare. His features remind me of his father's, Hades.

He smirks. "Everyone did... Heard you were a stripper in the Earth World."

I wave him off, sucking my teeth.

He leans more into me and picks my chin with his fingers. "You want to show me what you did there?"

My eyes travel up and down his body before a smirk runs across my lips. "Oh, please... You can't handle this."

Hell's Reaper

Ozzy cocks a brow as I reach over him and grab the bottle of liquor he is sipping. I take a swig before turning and moving away with the bottle. I glance back to see him smiling and staring.

Moving away, I find Hazen playing beer bong in the dining room with friends. I sit nearby and watch him. His smile is wide, and when he throws the last ball, he makes it in, and everyone shouts. Hazen looks at the crowd and meets my eyes. He smiles at me, and it makes my insides warm. *How dare he be this fine? Who is this hellhound, really?*

I move through the crowd to get to him, just as one of the girls says, "Let's play truth or dare!"

I try to turn away, but Hazen scoops me up by my waist. "Come on."

"Oh, I don't like high school games," I tease as a few from the party settle down on the dining room couch. The worst part is, I don't even know these people, only Hazen. My eyes glance around the room to make sure. Ozias is talking with Khazon, and they are in the range of the truth or dare. They could be included in this…

I stick to the outskirts of the circle as the girl dares some kid to drink some gross drink with raw eggs. Of course, he does it. Someone else dares someone to switch costumes with them.

"Asura, truth or dare," Miya challenges, eyes pinned on me. This is why I didn't want to play. She can dare me to do anything, like kiss Ledger and piss off Khazon, suck someone's dick, or even strip.

Because the devil didn't raise a bitch.

"Dare," I say, swigging my drink which has been passed between Hazen and me.

"I dare you to make out with Hazen on his lap for one minute," Miya says.

I lock eyes with Ledger. His jaw tightens, and Khazon stands over his shoulder, watching us. He's always there and watching.

*Oh well.* I stand, sliding into Hazen's lap, pushing away the liquor in his hands. My thighs are on each side of his, and I push my hair over my shoulder, looking at him. "Consent is key. Are you okay with this?"

"Like I'm going to fucking object," he says with a goofy smile.

"Timer," Amos says. "Starting…."

I run my hands up his chest and onto his neck, locking eyes with him. I lift his chin and move my lips to his. His lips shock me a bit, but I refuse to pull back.

"Now," Amos says.

His hands move, and I have no idea what happened to the bottle we were just drinking. His arm wraps around me, and his hand grabs my right hip, pulling me close.

Maybe this wasn't the best idea with an orgasm so close. Heat rushes to my core, and I can feel myself growing wet again just by how his lips move. He is amazingly good at kissing, and I can't help but wonder what his tongue would feel like between my legs. His other hand moves up to my face. I deepen the kiss, fisting his curls a bit. Our lips move together, and I forget about the party around us. Then he slips me his tongue, and of course, I let him in. Cheering roars around us, making him smirk against my lips. Idiots. Our tongues dance and swirl. Something about this kiss just feels natural and right. This feels like we've kissed before, instead of it being our first kiss.

Hazen's tongue wins our little war, and he pulls me closer. His cock is hardening against my core. At least I'm not the only one having this reaction.

"Time," Amos announces.

*That quick?* It takes me a second to pull back before the world comes crashing down and reality is back. Hazen smiles up at me, all goofy, and I push his head away. "Oh, shut it."

He chuckles, but I stay on his lap as the game continues. I look for Ledger and see he's gone. Is he mad now? We aren't even together. But I was his...

Hazen is way drunker than I am by the end of the night. It's hard to carry someone almost two feet taller than you and even more in these heels. But I managed to get him to the hound dorms and find his room number from his keys. I struggle to get the keys in with him on my shoulder, but I get it done. I throw him on the couch, which is definitely too small for him.

"Stay with me," he slurs, holding on to my hands.

I shush him in case he has roommates. "Go to bed."

He pulls me to him. "Can I have another kiss if I do?" Leaning in, I kiss his forehead, but it seems to make him happy for now. He smiles all wide and goofy. "Can I be one of your hounds?"

I pat his head. "If you remember this tomorrow, I will consider it."

"Oh! Let me give you my number." He tries to reach into his pocket but can't find it. I chuckle, reaching into his pocket to pull out his phone.

"You know," a voice says, making me jolt upward. "If you want to touch him like that, I'm sure if you ask when he's sober, he'll say yes."

I look up to see the dark-haired guy in the doorway of his room. He steps closer, and I see it's Jigsaw without his mask and shirt. I still, taking in his lips with scars around them and his pierced nose with the same scar. My eyes drop lower. He has abs running down his stomach to his deep V. Faint scars cover his whole chest, and his upper chest has tattoos over them, spreading all the way to his fingers.

My hips are tight with the edge I received earlier, but it grew worse by the night's end. Now it feels like I could just look at Jigsaw and burst. I open Hazen's phone and typed in my number. "He's drunk, and I would never take advantage of him."

Hazen groans. "Dang… Really?"

I smirk, standing and looking at Jigsaw. "Did we wake you?"

Jigsaw peers down at Hazen as he stops behind the couch. "Thought you were an intruder."

"And what would you have done with.... *that*?" I wave my hands all around his body.

"Do you not realize my whole body is a weapon?" His eyes narrow.

My eyes wander down to his crotch. He's wearing black sweats, and I can see the outline of his massive dick. A shiver runs down my spine thinking about it. *What a sexy weapon.*

He rolls his eyes. "I'd burn you from the inside out."

I look up, tilting my head. "Kinky."

He glares at me. "Go home before you get us in trouble, and Reapers are not allowed in the dorm when they have no hounds here."

I hold up my hands. "Next time, I'll leave him on the lawn."

"Fine by me," he grumbles.

We hold our gazes as I stand and move to the front door. "Hey, Jig?"

"Saw." He tries to correct me, moving to the front door.

"Whatever. Be my hound."

"No," he says instantly, opening the door for me.

I look up at his green eyes. "Why not?"

"Because I don't need that drama in my life."

I scoff. "I am not *drama*."

He cocks a brow. "How many hounds have you kissed or fucked so far?"

142

I stare at him, feeling anger rise in my chest. "You don't know me, and you can't judge my capability on that."

He chuckles. "I don't need a demon whose mind is only on fucking her hounds. *Leave.*"

I'm silent for a moment before moving. He closes the door on me, and I stand there for a moment. *Is that my only objective? Fucking my hounds? No, right. It's to stop a war from coming. I want to be stronger and better. How dare he? He doesn't even know me.* Jigsaw would be perfect for my group, though. His whole body is a weapon, and he would know how to use it. Hazen is going to be too drunk to remember what he asked. I think he's just as powerful, if not more, than Jigsaw. I shake my head and walk back to my dorm.

# Asura

Although we don't have classes the next day, I still get up two hours before breakfast starts, and I decided a morning run would be fun to burn off the sugary alcohol. Plus, what Inarian and Jigsaw keep saying is getting to me. *Am I taking this as seriously as everyone else?*

The campus is quiet during this hour of the morning. The people I see pretend I'm not alive; that's how I like it. Afterward, I do weightlifting in the gym. Halfway through my workout is when others start working out too, and I finish before any of them can even talk to me.

## Rune Hunt

My phone dings with a text just as I'm sipping my water and walking out of the gym.

**Unknown number:** We still have a deal?

I look around, trying to see if this is a joke.

**Me:** That deal is...?

**Unknown number:** That you kiss me when we are sober...

**Me:** Hazen? That wasn't the deal.

**Hazen:** Oh... Must have forgotten. Any who, can I be your hellhound?

**Me:** You actually remember that?

**Hazen:** Yes. And I can show you what I can do.

I bite my lip. I barely know this guy and want to do nothing more than fuck him. But I need a hound, and our chemistry might help us in the bonding ceremony.

**Me:** Training yard in twenty minutes.

I push open the gym doors, passing by someone. A cold shiver runs up my arm, creating goosebumps in its wake. I glance back to see a familiar icy, dark glare look back at me.

"Got to get up earlier, Inari," I tease.

"Don't call me that," he grumbles, walking inside.

Glancing back, I see him roll his broad shoulders to loosen them. My eyes wander to his nice ass in his sweats. *Jesus, these hounds will be the death of me.*

Hell's Reaper

I make my way to the training field quicker than Hazen. I don't have to wait long before the shirtless hound jogs my way.

"Good morning!" Hazen says with a smile. "Oh, why are *you* sweaty?"

I roll my eyes. "Good morning. I have questions. How good are you at fighting?"

He shrugs. "Ledger and I spar a lot, so I'd say I'm decent." He stretches upwards to the sky with a groan and a few cracks of his bones. His muscles ripple and stretch with him.

"Would you be willing to teach me?"

He raises a brow.

"I can't learn in that class; I'm only learning how Inarian fights. I need more training."

He nods. "Yeah, I'd be willing to kick your ass a few times."

I chuckle. "And your power is… electricity?"

He nods, moving to me and running a finger over the back of my hand. It shocks me enough to pull back with a gasp, and my nerves awaken in my body.

"How powerful is that?"

Hazen kneels, pressing a hand into the ground. White lightning bolts glow behind his tan skin and enter the ground from his palm. It rumbles the ground, bouncing between the plants' roots until it hits a tree that begins to spark.

I smirk. "Careful."

He pulls back, white veins popping from his bronze skin. "I have enough volts in my body to kill at least ten people, then I have to recharge."

I watch as the tree calms down and stops smoking. "I haven't seen many hellhounds in action."

He rolls his shoulders. "Want to see my hound?"

"Yes!" Joy leaps inside of me. I've only seen a few hounds, including Ledger's fire hound.

"Set up a target for me," he says, pointing at the equipment by the training yards wall. The field reminds me of a football field from high school—a human high school—with fewer field goals and lines. Most people run around the track while others use nearby equipment from the shed. He kicks off his sneakers and begins pulling down his pants, but not his boxers.

"Hazen!" I don't advert my eyes.

He chuckles. "I will be naked if I don't do this."

Cracking fills the air, all his muscles contort, and his limbs lengthen. He drops to his knees, face shifting until he resembles a wolf. His hound is just as big as Ledger's, but he has white fur covering his whole body with glowing blue marks, which I can only assume is his magic. Hellhounds are normally seven-feet-tall in their human *and* hound forms.

Resisting the urge to pet him, I move in front of him, putting a target bullseye in his line of sight. I step aside, but he jerks his head, telling me to move more.

Hell's Reaper

Moving further away, I see his shoulders stiffen as he reels back before releasing a giant roar. A bolt of glowing gray electricity flies from his mouth and hits the target, and it explodes in a million pieces, flying throughout the air. My eyes widen as I look at the scene in front of me. He's powerful, just as powerful as Ledger and his Hellfire.

After a moment, Hazen shifts back with a groan, stretching his limbs and shaking them out. I pick up his sweats and hold them out for him. I try so hard not to look, but at the last second, I glance down. His cock is thick and hefty, with veins leading to the swollen tip, and I'm not even sure he's hard.

He chuckles, sliding on his pants. "So?"

*Enormous...* "Uh." I blink, trying to remember what we were talking about. "I think you are very powerful. I also think that we will work well together."

He smiles. "Yeah? I mean... after the bonding ceremony, we still have the choice to separate."

My eyes narrow. *Why would he say that? If we bond successfully, I want to stay with him. Unless he's like Inarian and had a reaper without being successful.* "How come you don't have a reaper? Your magic could be so useful."

His hands twitch, but I can't tell if he means to do that. "I just haven't been able to find one that works with me. I feel like you, and I can be good together."

I bite my lip. "We will see."

He smiles. "Hey, do you want to go get breakfast?"

148

I glance down, seeing the outline of his…
"You, uh, need clothing."

He looks down at himself. "What? You don't like?"

I snort, walking away. I don't need to tell him I love it; *He knows.* "Meet at the mess hall? Are you going to sit with Ledger and the others?"

He nods. "Yeah, but I don't have to."

"No. I need intel, and I need to know if he's pissed at us."

"For?"

"For kissing." I freeze. "He and I kind of… had a moment in the bathroom."

Hazen snorts. "I know, I smelled him on you… I'm sure he's not pissed. The kiss was just a dare, *right*?" He bumps me, moving to the hellhound dorm. My eyes fall to his ass for a few steps before turning to the mess hall and getting breakfast. I doubt Amos will be here by how drunk she was yesterday. I grab what I usually get, turning around and locking eyes with Ledger at his usual table.

He clenches his jaw and looks away.

"Men." I huff, rolling my eyes

I see Inarian sitting alone, reading a book; he's a bit sweaty from his morning workout. I move to his table, sitting across from him, and he doesn't even bother to look up.

"I have a hellhound."

He glances up, "Feel bad for that poor fuck."

I roll my eyes. "You know, Inari, I—"

"Don't call me that."

"I'm going to be the strongest one here. You should hop on this before you lose the chance to." I ignore his comment.

He takes a sip of his water. "You have potential."

My brow cocks, and a smirk curls on my lips. "Was that a compliment?"

"You have potential... but your mind is in other places."

I wave him off. "No." *He's not wrong. My mind is on home and what I'm going to do to save it.*

He sets down his book. "Why do you want to be the best, Asura?"

I feel cold when he says my name. "Uh..."

"You just want it because you've always been the best for no reason. You strive for acceptance because you never got it as a kid."

My brows pull together as I chuckle. "You know nothing about me. I may be the heir, but trust me, I've been accepted by everyone in my life. I don't want acceptance and can care less about what people think about me."

"Then why do you want to be the best, Asura? Because you want dick from your hounds, or?"

"Right, because to you, I'm just the princess who only cares about dick, yet I wouldn't touch yours with a ten-foot pole, asshole."

Rune Hunt

He lets out a chuckle. "Yeah? Thank God. I would never have someone as weak as you on my dick."

*Show him weak...* The demonic voice in my head makes me smile.

"I'm going to win you over one day." I stand, grabbing my energy drink. I look at the book and realize I have read it. "He *dies* at the end."

He closes the book, staring up at me. "Really? Are you actually being petty like that?"

Walking away, I feel his cold stare on me, but I don't look back. I won't be weak for long. I'm not even sure how I'm going to get stronger. I don't know much about fighting anymore. I need help.

At the club, I used to practice a lot when I was in moods like this. The focus on doing something made me feel better. Now I can't dance like I used to. Now it's fighting, but I can't learn without doing the real thing. I fell on my ass from the pole many times, but I still got up and tried again. I'll show Inarian how strong I can really be.

"Are you nervous?" Amos's shoulder bumps me at the telum ceremony as we stand in line to take a seat later that night.

I shrug. "I hope I get a small dagger and have to use that for the rest of my life."

"Some have," she says, entering the assembly room that holds at least two thousand people.

151

## Hell's Reaper

"New reapers over there," a teacher directs me, handing me a blue chip. *Enhancement chip.*

"Do I need to take this?" Nerves enter my chest. I know how the ceremony works, and I should have prepared for this. You take a blue enhancement chip which enhances your powers to a level that will help you. You chant a spell, and *boom!* The weapon is yours. But part of me was hoping I could get away without using it.

He nods. "You need the extra strength for the telum."

Hesitating, I shove the chip into my mouth, and it dissolves quickly, and I can already feel it rushing through my veins. I look at Amos, who is directed the other way, and she sends me a thumbs up. She already had her telum from last year, a reaper scythe, which is surprisingly rare.

Glancing around, I see Killian is one of the first people in the first row, basically jumping with joy. Slowly the assembly room grows louder and louder with each group of people that enters. I try not to focus on anything but the thought of my demon coming out to play.

I remember the mage telling my father what would happen when I took any type of magical chips, including enhancement chips.

"Settle down," the dean, Dean Moon, says when he enters the stage. "Good morning."

Some mutter it back.

Rune Hunt

"Today, we will be doing the telum ceremony. A ceremony where first-year reapers are awarded a weapon for their journey of becoming Soul Reapers. As you know, souls power almost everything in the Shadow World, including the electricity in this school. It is a highly demanding job here, and you will have opportunities that few have ever had.

"Now, I expect the upperclassmen to be on their best behavior as they concentrate. One by one, the reapers will come up, shift into their demon form if they haven't, and then reach for their weapon. The enhancement chips enhance their powers, and most newcomers will not be strong enough to pull them out without the chips. Slowly, you will learn how to do that over the next few months. But the chips will bring out your demon form..."

*I get to come out?* The demon in my head says.

*Fuck.* I swallow. Typically, a reaper's body is fused with a demon, which is a big difference. She's a different person, and I have no control over her when she takes over. My medicine stops her from coming out.

My heart picks up. *Will you behave?*

*Maybe...*

*Then you don't get to come out, Circe.*

I hear her suck her teeth. *I'll behave, Asura... I promise. I never get to come out. I want to show them who we can be and who not to fuck with.*

*Just behave.*

153

## Hell's Reaper

It was hard to keep her inside, but we have gotten to the point in our relationship that we understand that we can't be mean to everyone and kill them because they were mean to us.

Circe sometimes forgets that.

People start going up and taking their chance at pulling a weapon out of thin air, or as the dean called it, "our personal locker."

Circe makes my legs shake with anticipation.

I put my hands on my knees, trying to stop the movement. "Stop it," I growl, fixing my eyes on the stage. Glancing around, I meet eyes with Hazen. He tilts his head, brows pulling together. *How can he tell something is wrong?*

I shake my head.

*Sorry! You push me down so much that I missed being this close to the surface,* Circe speaks in my head.

*Because you hurt people.*

*Oops.*

155

# Hell's Reaper

Killian is next to get onto the stage, calling on his demon form. His demon is like our father's, with dark red skin, pitch-black eyes, and horns curling from his head. Then he reaches out and pulls the ax from the air so easily. His blade is hot and red like it's been in a fire. He smirks, eying it before putting it back.

I clap the loudest, smiling, and even Circe shouts in my head, *We love him. We are so proud.*

It takes a while, but butterflies eat my stomach when we are close to being up. I hate shifting and giving her control, and I never know how she will act. My hands shake as I get close to going up on stage.

I lock eyes with my brother, and he throws a thumb up. *He doesn't know how this feels; his demon isn't a whole different person.*

I try not to look at anyone. Seeing Ledger will make me want to leave.

*Who is Ledger?*

My eyes find him almost instantly in the crowd. His red eyes meet mine, and he lifts his chin.

*Tall, dark, and handsome? That's Ledger. Mhm, have you fucked him yet? Will he fuck me?*

*No. Stop this.*

My eyes move to Khazon, who looks… *worried*. His eyes are soft for the first time in a while, and I can't help but think he's concerned about me. I know he knows what I am going through and how Circe is in my head. Khazon was always there for me through all the weird psychotic breaks where Circe forced me down. He was always there to comfort me

156

and make me feel better. He was there for the side effects of the meds, and he was... he was always there for me.

Miya grabs his hand and holds it, and my eyes drop. *Now he hates me.*

*Who is that fucking bitch?* Circe growls, almost coming up like vomit.

I swallow. *Circe.*

*Khazon is ours. He was* our *first love. Ours.* Rage enters my chest, and I can't decipher if it's hers or mine. I'm the Princess of Hell. I should be able to control my fucking demon as Killian can, and I shouldn't struggle and have to take medicine to control her.

My leg bounces.

*Kill her.*

I freeze. Intrusive thoughts that Circe *will* go through with... I've almost killed Soul Reapers because of her. I mean, they shouldn't have hurt me or touched me, but still.

*How dare she fucking touch him? He's ours, not hers. Hurt her. Show her how fucking crazy you can be.*

I stand slowly.

*Good girl.*

Khazon's eyes meet mine once more before moving out of the auditorium. *I can't be in there.* I can't let them know how fucking crazy I can be. "Go back there and show them who is in charge," Circe's dark voice breaks from my throat as soon as I step

157

outside. It's harsh and rough.

I need to go back to my dorm and grab my medicine.

"She took him from us and—"

"No, she didn't!" I snap, grabbing my hair. "I left, and you know this!"

"You shouldn't talk to yourself," a voice says from behind me, making me whirl around. A fae girl sits there smoking a cigarette and looking at the sky.

"Mind your own business," Circe says.

A smile runs on her lips, piercings on her lip shifting with her curling mouth. She stands, necklace chain clanking, her pointed ears sag from the weight of her plugs. Her narrow almond-shaped eyes move to me.

Her full lips are glossy pink with a piercing on the bottom one. She has a septum piercing and a pretty pink highlighted nose that reaches out to her high cheekbones. Pink hearts are scattered across her cheeks. She has black wing eyeliner, and her brows are filled in with white, with four dots above them. Her hair is long, hanging down to her hips, but her bangs are pushed behind her pointed ears. She wears black cargo pants with a belt, a chain that hangs, and black boots.

"Oh, you're an elf," I mutter. My head spins, and so does the world around me.

The elf grabs my arms and holds me. "Whoa. Are you okay, demon?"

I stand back up, fixing myself. "Uh…Sorry."

She throws the cigarette down. "Come sit down. Here." She helps me to the bench. "You don't often shift, huh?"

I shake my head. "It's a lot sometimes."

She touches my hands, and it's then I realize my hands are shaking. "Are you okay?"

I pull back. "Yeah. I just… I need to go to my dorm." I take a deep breath. "Thank you. I'll be okay."

"Are you sure? Should I walk you?"

I shake my head. "Thank you." Slowly, I take my time getting back to the dorm. The stairs inside feel like the longest trip up. The world is spinning, and Circe is trying to gain control to stop me. Inside the room, my vision blurs. My body aches as if someone has beaten me over and over. *Circe is so close to the surface.* I rush inside, moving straight to my bathroom and opening the medicine cabinet.

But the cabinet is empty.

*My medicine is gone.* My brows pull together and my hand pushes aside anything in the way. "Where—"

"Looks like you misplaced it," Circe comments.

She knows I'd never do that. I pull out my phone, ignoring the texts from people flooding in, and dial my father.

"Hey, diaboli," my dad says, answering the phone.

"Can you come and get me?" I ask, eyes burning with tears. "I can't—I can't find my medicine, and Circe is—"

He doesn't even let me finish. "Be there in five. Stay on the phone."

I drop to my knees, my body crumbling with the pain. Circe has been fighting me this whole time. Suddenly, my vision blurs, and all the will I have is gone.

# Circe

"Asura? Asura? Are you—" the devil starts, making me roll my eyes at him.

I snatch the phone up from the floor. "No, Father, she isn't here anymore."

He lets out a sigh. "Don't you dare do anything that will harm her."

I scoff. "This is my body, too." I get to my feet, stretching for the first time in so many years. It gets cramped being trapped in someone else's body and mind. I look at myself in the mirror.

I look so much different in *her* body. My black horns curl through her silver curls, and her bronze skin has completely changed to my lilac purple. My hands and arms have silver swirls of magic rushing through them. My face looks exactly like Asura's, and although

160

she's gorgeous, it's not *mine*. My tail wraps around my body and flicks something off the counter by accident. It's been a while since my tail has been out and free.

"Circe, don't hurt her," her father says. "Just give her the medicine back."

Rolling my eyes, I run a hand over my curves. "Someone else took them, and I had no idea she didn't have them."

"Someone took them?" The voice echoes in the room through the phone. I twist to see the devil standing tall as ever in a suit. He's never been my cup of tea, but I guess the silver fox would make others go wild.

I hang up the phone, setting it on the counter. "The sweet smell of flowers is right here. Magic... Maybe a witch or mage."

He moves into the bathroom and inhales.

*Asura can't smell like I can.*

"Seems too weak to be a mage... You think someone stole her medicine?"

I nod.

"Why?"

Shrugging, I twirl to the mirror. "Why else? Someone might know."

The devil's eyes darken. "How?"

"Ask your daughter. Maybe she told that hot hellhound, or maybe Khazon told his ugly ass girlfriend."

"Circe, let Asura have her spot back."

My eyes move to him in the mirror, and a smirk runs across my lip. "Your daughter is weak. Do you really think you can stop me from taking the throne from—"

"Stop it!" he snaps.

I whirl around. "She's weak. She's human. She's—"

He grabs my face and presses his palm into my mouth. I feel the heat of Hell crossing my face. "I told you to shut the fuck up."

I blink at him, feeling his magic starting to weaken me. I might not be as strong as the Devil, but I know he hates using magic on his precious heir. I pull back, huffing. "My deal with you is dwindling."

"She's not ready for the throne yet."

"You and I both know it will happen." My eyelids grow heavy. "Sooner than later, right, *Dad*? When are they coming?"

"I don't know. I need her to be stronger. I can't…" His eyes soften, looking down at me. "I need her to be stronger. Help her."

I shrug. "No. I can't even if I wanted to. I'm always drugged into silence. Scared, I'm going to tell her the truth about the deal?"

He nods. "You can't shut up to save your life. Unless you are asleep."

My eyes close as his voice grows further and further away as his magic completely takes over. *Fuck him and his stupid sleeping magic.*

# Asura

Something hard lands on my stomach, earning a groan that wakes me up from my slumber.

"What the—" I grab at the small body on top of me and open my eyes.

"Watch the language!"

I know the voice instantly, causing me to grip him, move him up, and plant kisses all over his cheek. Fenric tries to pull back, squealing like a little pig.

Killian throws open the curtains, making my room brighter and making me hiss. My head is pounding, and my eyes burn. "Get up. You slept for like sixteen hours, and your boyfriends won't stop *fucking* texting me."

"Who?" I scoff.

"Khazon, Ledger, and Hazen. They are all fucking annoying. Khazon tried to stop by, but Dad refused to let him enter your room. What happened to you? One second you were there, the next you were gone."

I sat up, barely remembering much after I got home. I just remember being in the bathroom looking for my medicine. I had taken them that morning, knowing where I put them. But they were gone, and Circe took control. "Nothing. Don't worry about it, buddy." They know my demon takes more energy than theirs, but they don't fully understand what I am.

Killian looks down. "Still, you might want to text Ledger back before he storms the castle."

I roll my eyes. "Ledger doesn't really like me right now."

"Why?" Fen asks. "I like him, but who's Hazen?"

I push him onto the bed. "Hazen is my hound, and Ledger is—"

"Jealous," Killian finishes.

"No."

He sends me a look. "The motherfucker is jealous."

I roll my eyes. "Whatever. I'll call him."

Fenric jumps from the bed. "I'm making lunch. You want some?"

"Yes, and it better be really good, or we're going to have to resort to eating... you!" I jump after him, but he runs out of the room before I can even grab him.

Killian moves to the door. "How long have you been on these meds?" When I look up at him, he says, "Dad told me... Where did they come from?"

Sighing, I say, "I've been on them for about four and a half years. A witch doctor made them for me after I hurt some people when Circe took over."

He nods. "And they are safe? They work?"

I nod. "Enchantment chips counteract the pills, so... But other than that, they've helped a lot and made me feel normal."

He punches my arm. "How can anyone like you really be 'normal?'"

"Get out before I eat you too."

"With your appetite, I believe it, fatty."

I kick his ass on the way out and close my door. Grabbing my phone from my nightstand, I see all the messages I've missed from Khazon, Hazen, Amos, and even Ledger. I call Amos and tell her I am fine but don't give her any other details.

Hazen picks up instantly when I dial his number. "Hi!" He then clears his throat. "Hello. Hi."

I giggle. "Hi, Hazen."

"You disappeared... Are you okay?" His voice lowers a bit.

"I'm all right. I went home. I was just exhausted."

"Okay, cool... So, just ignore my fifty messages about me freaking out."

Hazen picked up on something being wrong so quickly. He might make a great partner for me.

"Are you going to be okay, princess?"

I smile. Hazen says it is so much sweeter than Ledger. I remember our kiss and how turned on he made me. "I... uh... have to go to call my other boyfriends."

"Oh, so this isn't just a reaper and hound relationship? Mhm... I thought you liked me by the way you smelled and—"

"Goodbye, Haze!" I cut him off.

"Text me so I know you don't die."

"Don't tell me what to do. I'll die if I want to, fucker."

He laughs as we hang up. I bite my lip, thinking maybe I should call him back and just talk to him. *He did send me fifty text messages. How insane?*

My phone rings, making me look down to see "Ledge" on the caller ID.

"Hello?"

"How dare you call him first when I am more worried than he is?" he teases.

"Why are you worried?"

He stops speaking, and I hear Hazen laugh in the background. *So, they are together.*

"I'm fine. Thank you for checking in on me."

"Yeah," he says. "You're welcome. I'm, uh, probably going to see you later."

"Huh?"

166

He sighs. "The king invited us to dinner... Khazon and his hounds."

I throw myself back on the bed. "Ugh. How fun."

"Tell me about it."

*I have so much to say and ask, but how do I even start. Do you hate me? Our conversations have never been like this. We are always talking about something; it's never quiet or dull.*

"I'm glad to know you're okay. Uh... See you later, okay?"

"Mhm, Bye, Ledge."

"Bye." He hangs up, and I sit back up and throw myself back down. Why did that make my chest tighten painfully? With a huff, I get up, put on music, and move to the bathroom. After taking more of my meds, I begin getting ready for the day, or at least lunch. For dinner, I feel like Dad might make me dress up.

As quickly as I walk into the dining room, I hear my father's deep voice. "Better not be wearing that to dinner, Asura."

"Is this dinner, Dad, or lunch?"

He peers at me over his tablet. "Sassy today, huh?"

"You invited Khazon to dinner?" I ask, sitting next to Killian as Fenric comes out with soup and a grilled cheese sandwich.

"Yes, is that a problem?"

I meet his eyes. Dad doesn't care about my problems.

"Khazon and her aren't friends right now," Derrick mutters, eating his soup.

"Shut up!" I snap.

"Why? You guys grew up together," my dad whines, hands up like he's saying "why" with them.

"Because she fucked Ledger, his hellhound, and his best friend, Hazen."

I gasp. "Do not fucking lie like that!"

"Well, maybe if you weren't such a fucking who—"

"Watch your mouth!" my father growls, his demon threatening to come to the surface, making the room grow hotter. "Don't call your sister that, whether she slept with them or not."

Derrick scoffs, pushing back from the table and leaving.

I wait until I hear his door upstairs slamming before I speak. "I haven't slept with all of them; I'm more focused on finding hounds and growing as a Soul Reaper."

My father nods, looking down at his tablet. "Are they nice guys, at least?"

"Dad!" I glare at him, and Fenric giggles.

He holds up his hands in defense. "Just curious."

It's silent, and I go to take a bite of my sandwich.

"Are you inviting Hazen to dinner?"

I groan. "No. I didn't even think about that. He's probably busy." I bite my lip. Maybe I should ask him. But I barely know him. He could be a murderer, but he's too soft for that.

The doorbell rings—yes, we have a doorbell since Dad insisted we got one.

"Fen, get it!" My father shouts from the kitchen.

I glance at Fenric, who looks a little upset that he couldn't finish the table setting. He took his time to make the napkins into two devil horns. "I'll get it," I say, winking to Fenric and moving to the front door.

The clanking of my heels against the tile floor fills my chest with power. Grabbing the handle and opening the door, it groans like it's from a horror movie before I see Khazon and his three hounds behind him.

I smile sweetly, moving to the side.

"Do you not answer calls anymore?" Khazon grumbles.

"Are you ever not miserable, *Death*?"

He glares at me, entering the house. I must admit that I love his suit and how it fits him. The sleeves are tight around his muscles, and the pants cup his ass. Not that I was looking.

I glance at Ledger, whose eyes go up and down my body without trying to hide it. He's wearing a black sweater and matching slacks with a chain on the side. His fingers are in his pockets, and his boots clank

169

as he passes me. His ass... *Ugh, so good.* I let the
others enter, not even remembering their names. I
follow behind, letting my heels echo. The dress I have
on is black and silky. It's mid-thigh and has the back
cut out with spaghetti straps holding it up.

My father enters the room just as we do. He has
an apron on with flour, covering his clothing.

"Hello, sir," Khazon says, grabbing my father's
hand when he holds it out.

"Oh, please, don't call me sir. I've known you
for too long." My father shakes his hand, though.
Holding his hand out for Ledger. "And you guys are?"

"I'm Ledger," he answers, taking his hand and
giving a firm handshake.

One apparently my father likes because he
sends me a quick look. "Ledger! I heard a lot about
you."

*Oh god!*

Ledger's brows bounce. "I hope good things,
sir."

My father introduces himself to the others
while I move to the bar to get a drink, anything to get
the edge off.

"Should you be drinking right now?" Ledger's
voice comes out more as a whisper.

I cock a brow, looking up. Even in these heels,
he's still much taller. "So, you don't want one?"

"I'll take one," he mutters, running a hand
through his dark hair, and I grab a glass before pouring
another. I give it to him, sipping mine. The warmth of

the whiskey hits my stomach. "So, you and Hazen, huh?"

I freeze. "Ledge…"

"He's going to be your hellhound, right?"

I glance up. *He's not talking about the kiss or anything? Should I apologize?* We weren't dating, but I also kissed him the same week. One week in, and the drama is a lot—my own fault. I have never been in a relationship with anyone because of my indecisiveness. Khazon asked me out once, but deep down, I knew I had feelings for him and Ozias, Hades's son, and I wasn't willing to lose both. I wanted both, though. "Ledger." I lower my voice, glancing at my family. "About that kiss. It was just a dare."

He sips his whiskey, red eyes looking down at me. "And the dancing?"

I curse myself. I had forgotten that Hazen and I danced. "Ledge…"

"Come sit and eat!" my father says.

Ledger's lips curls in a smile. "Come on," he says, letting me move away first. Like a stupid gentleman, he moves my chair and allows me to sit down before helping me push it in. Then he sits across from me, Khazon and Killian on either side. Fen and one of the other hellhounds are next to me. Dad is at the head, in between Fen and Killian.

"So, Ledger, how did you become Khazon's hellhound?" my father asks as the fae staff begins serving us.

"Thank you," I mutter to the staff.

171

"I actually wasn't his first choice, and I think he just settled for me," Ledger says, bumping Khazon.

*How good was their relationship? It had to be good, right? To do the bonding ceremony?*

Khazon laughs. "I wanted a powerful fire hound, so I got one. Your brother was taken, though."

*I didn't know Ledger had a brother.*

"Punching me in the face isn't how you should have got me," Ledger says, smiling down at the food.

My father chuckles. "I remember my hounds, and I punched one too; he had a mouth on him."

Khazon nods, sipping his drink. "That's Ledger."

Ledger chuckles.

The dinner goes on with all of them talking. I can tell my father likes Ledger the most because he keeps questioning him, genuinely interested. It got me to learn more about him which I enjoyed.

"Asura, would you mind helping me with the dessert?" my father asks as I sip the last drop of my second whiskey.

I just nod; this is not out of the norm. My father likes to bake… Yeah, my father likes to bake. *The devil.* I stand, smoothing my skirt down and following him into the kitchen.

"I like him," my father whispers.

I roll my eyes. "Did you know Khazon forbade me to see him?"

My father gasps. "Well, that's because he loves you."

*So, I've heard.* "It's just not going to work, Dad, so…"

"Because this Hazen kid is in the picture now?" my father questions. He loves drama and acting like he knows the situation.

I snort. "Yeah, sure."

"Do you… like him?"

"Which one?" I tease; I like them all. I like Ledger, Hazen, Jigsaw, and even Inarian's rude ass. *Although Hazen and Ledger are the only ones that checked in on me after…* "Hey, Dad?"

He looks up at me.

"What happened when you picked me up? Did she… say anything?"

He looks down at the pie. "No, not really. Why?"

I shrug. "Just wondering. You've been acting weird."

He cocks a brow. "How?"

"You mentioned your hellhounds. You never do that."

It's silent as he stares down at the food. "You don't like learning about my hounds? I know I'm old, but I thought it could help you get your hounds by talking about mine."

"Were the hounds I've talked about in your vision?"

He smiles lightly at me. "The faces were blurry. Sorry, diaboli. Help me carry this stuff out."

I nod.

# Asura

The other two of Khazon's hounds, Andrew and Eames, end up leaving early because Eames got too drunk. My father wouldn't shut up while talking to Ledger, so I ended up saying goodbye and going upstairs. The whole night, I texted Hazen and updated him. He spoke to me about it and joked around a lot. Maybe I should have invited him… But I didn't want to make Ledger even madder at me, although it doesn't seem like he is now.

I move to the bathroom in my room, starting the tub with hot water. I kick off my heels before grabbing the straps on my dress, about to strip.

Feeling eyes burning into me, I look up in the mirror and jolt when I see Ledger's enormous body taking up most of the doorway. His red eyes meet my own.

"Can I help you?" I say in a small voice.

He looks mad. A muscle in his jaw clenches and his eyes are narrowed into slits.

"Ledger?" I question, turning around to look up at him. He towers over me, and how his red eyes move over me makes me feel small and like his prey. *He* is the predator. His hand wraps around my neck. Fear runs through me, but it also feels euphoric. His touch is hot, yet his steel rings are cold against my skin.

"Seeing you with Hazen didn't piss me off."

"But you left and—"

His fist tightens, and I gulp on my words. "Because it turned me on."

*It turned him on. Is that why he met me in the bathroom after Hazen and I were together?* Heat swirls in my stomach.

"I liked watching you dance on him and the sweet smell you gave off." He begins to back me up until my back hits the counter. I gasp, grabbing out for it. "Just watching you make out with him made it so much harder not to fuck you right there. Get naked."

I smirk, feeling defiant. "Make me."

He cocks a dark brow. "Are..." He growls deeply and steps closer to the point where I must push myself onto the counter to avoid getting crushed between him and the sink. "Take it off, now."

Slowly, I lower my strap only a little bit, my fingers lingering against my skin.

175

He groans, grabbing the fabric of the dress. I feel heat kissing my skin lightly as he melts away the fabric. I gasp, careful not to get burned. "You think you're in charge because you're the Princess of Hell?"

I chuckle, grabbing his shirt and pulling his face to mine. Our lips are so close to each other that they're almost touching. "I'm dominant because you are looking for very submissive right now. Wanting me so badly that you are willing to beg for it."

"I'm not begging," he grumbles.

I grasp his throat, holding him reasonably where I can lift and spread my legs. I can feel the wetness between my thighs, *knowing* he can smell it. "You left me unsatisfied, and I didn't appreciate that."

His eyes move down to my crotch. "Did he fuck you?"

"No," I answer. "I wish. I would have come so hard after you edged me."

He mouths, "Oh fuck," eyes rolling to the ceiling.

I run a finger between my pussy's lips, drawing his attention back to me. Then I run the wetness right over the crotch of his pants. His cock twitches. "How badly do you want to taste me?"

His eyes snap to mine.

I repeatedly stick a finger through my soaking wet folds before bringing them up. His lips part and I know he wants a taste, so I give in. His tongue wraps around my fingers as soon as they get close to his mouth. He sucks on them, moaning.

"On your knees," I order, pulling my fingers back. He just stares at me; I grip his neck. "*Now.*"

Ledger grumbles, but he gets onto his knees before me, eyes locked on my pussy. He's still so tall on his knees, but fuck, he looks so good below me.

I move to the edge, running a hand through his short black hair.

His ringed finger pushes aside my thong before he lets out a breath. My pussy pulses at the warmth of the breath tickling it. I want it as much as he does. He leans in and tries to lick, and even though I'm shaking hard, I grip his hair and stop him. "Finish what you started."

He let out a chuckle. "Asura. Don't play with me."

I smirk. "Play? I don't play... We are just getting started."

He grips my thighs, pulling me to his face. But instead of licking me, he sinks his canine teeth into my thigh.

I gasp as the pain brings me pleasure. *How dare he?*

His tongue flicks across the indent of his teeth. "Let me eat you, baby."

"Please," I say as I breathe out.

He wastes no time, tilting my body back and diving into my pussy.

I gasp at the warmth of his tongue as he has no problem finding my nerve nub. The pleasure running through me is something that I've never felt before.

177

Then again, it's not every day that a seven-foot hellhound with a long tongue eats me out. Last time he left me on the edge, and I have stayed on edge since, aching for his warmth.

His tongue goes deep into my hole, twirling inside of me and making me want to close my legs. But Ledger holds them up tightly.

His mouth is so warm, and he eats me like he's never eaten before. I rake my fingers in his hair, pulling on it when I get to the back of his head.

His red eyes flutter open and lock onto mine. It sends a heat of pleasure to my core. *Damn it. I'm not going to fucking last.*

I drop my head back, rolling my hips and chasing my high. "Oh, Ledger," I say softly. I am still aware that Khazon might be here, and my family is nearby.

He reaches up, fingers brushing my hard nipples before he reaches out and grabs my head, guiding it forward.

He wants me to watch him make me come. I bite my lip, heels digging into his back. "Please, don't stop." *Look at me begging. Fuck it. I need to come.*

I try not to look away as my legs shake around his head. My moans grow as the pressure builds inside of me. Then that feeling comes. An orgasm that is so close, I can't help but fuck his face. My hips move, catching the high.

But he moves, stopping me.

Rune Hunt

His arms wrap around my waist, and he lifts me
into the air. I grab his head, gasping and stilling myself
so I don't fall, but he has a tight grip on me. He moves
to a wall, pushing me against it and continuing his
assault. The angle is head-on, and his tongue is precise
now that he knows how to flick his tongue to get me to
orgasm. His hand captures one of my breasts,
squeezing my nipple. My eyes roll back.

I hold his head close, feeling the orgasm riddle
in my hips. I arch, but he keeps me held up. He could
drop me at any fucking moment, but I don't care as
long as I get this orgasm.

Then it comes.

It hits me so hard; I'm panting and crying out. I
feel the rush of juices hit his face and wet my thighs.

"Fuck." I gasp, trying to steady my breathing
and my shaking body. Like I weighed nothing, Ledger
lifted me from his shoulders. My legs shake like Jell-
O, so I cling to the wall to hold me up. From his nose
down, it's soaking wet. His long tongue rolls out and
licks the wetness from above his lip. *Fuck.*

"Turn," he orders.

I hesitate. "Uh."

He growls, moving me from the wall and
turning me against the counter. He positions me until
my hips touch it. "Listen before *you* are punished. I let
you be dominant *once,* and you won't get another
chance."

Hell's Reaper

My eyes widened. My head is in such a bad lust fog from him eating me out that I can barely come up with anything to say back.

I watch him in the mirror move to the tub, shut it off and shred his sweater that is soaked with my juices. My eyes move over his back, taking in the ridges of muscles and faint scars. They were battle scars, but I want to add new ones of my own.

I hear his buckle as he turns around. One swift moment and it's off. His gaze moves to my ass as he grips his belt. "One day, I will punish you so badly; your whole ass will be blue."

My core clenches as I think about it. *I want it more than anything right now.*

He then kicks off his shoes and drops his pants and boxers, and I catch a glimpse of his massive, long dick. "Jesus..." I mutter as his hand rubs up and down his long length.

"Something wrong, Asura?" he asks in a husky voice, stepping behind me.

"Uh… It's slightly scary how big you are."

He chuckles, running a heavy hand up my spine and then back to my ass. His heat is warm and inviting but an illusion as he slams into me. It takes the air out of my lungs and makes my body tense. The wetness I had dripping down my legs and soaking my pussy didn't help as any type of lube.

"You can't handle it again?" He chuckles, rubbing my ass and back.

"Do you even know how vaginas work? I need a second," I grit out, willing myself to relax. I move my hips slightly. Each inch I move feels somewhat better than the last, and soon, I'm accustomed to his length and thickness.

He leans over my back, pulling my head up so I can look at him in the mirror. "I'm not even all the way in," he whispers into the shell of my ear.

It runs lust through me. "Fuck."

His free hand grabs my hip, and slowly, he pulls out of me and then shoves slowly back inside of me.

I close my eyes as he hits every single good wall inside of me. It doesn't take him long to start pounding me. His first harsh thrust makes me open my eyes and draws out a loud moan.

His hand claps over my mouth. "Shut the fuck up, princess."

My eyes move to his.

"Take it, Asura," he growls, jaw tightening. The pleasure makes my legs shake; if his hand weren't on my sternum, I'd be putty on the counter. "Fuck." He pounds into me over and over, building me up until every single one of my limbs tingles.

"Fuck, please don't stop." But it comes out muffled.

His hand tightens around my mouth. "Look at me."

Hell's Reaper

I open my eyes, not realizing they are closed. I get lost in his red eyes; It's only him and me together right now; nothing else matters.

"Look at me while you come, baby," he says with a moan. Sweat clings to his skin, and veins bulge in his arms and chest.

He's close, too, lips parting with moans.

I move his hand from my lips. "Come for me, Ledger."

His red eyes narrow. "A—"

"Please, Ledge, please come for me."

His pounding quickens and hardens. His hand moves to my throat when my eyes roll back, and he makes my back arch back. "Look at me," he growls.

I meet his eyes, trying to cry out, but his hand tightens around my throat. My body stiffens, and every single nerve in my body turns hot with his touch. With a silent cry, the orgasm hits me hard with his last thrust, tears drawing into my eyes, but I don't close them. He clenches his jaw, and his dick twitches, spilling inside me.

"Good girl." He breathes, letting me go.

I gasp hard, dropping my head. My silver hair clings to my face.

"Should I have given you a safe word?" he asks, pulling out from my pussy. I feel the cum dripping out of me, but he pushes it back in with two fingers.

My spit coats my dry throat as I let out a sigh. "No… I'm okay." Slowly, I push myself off the counter and teeter off balance.

He lets out a tired chuckle, grabbing my shoulder and stilling me. "I got you, baby."

# Asura

I roll over in the massive bed, looking up at Ledger. He stayed the night, and we cuddled even though he was a human heater. Okay, I forced him to cuddle me. Me, a five-foot-five woman, was cuddling with a seven-foot hellhound shifter…

A smile curls on my lips.

Ledger looks so peaceful when he sleeps, definitely not the angry fire hound like he is when he's awake. My hand runs over his muscular chest, touching all his faint scars, and they don't look huge, just tiny ones. *I thought hellhounds were supposed to heal themselves…*

My fingers run down his chest to the riddle of his abs. Hellhounds train and train at birth to become protectors for Soul Reaper, and I can only imagine the type of training Ledger does.

Then I glance down, seeing the tent of a boner. He's so big. *Are all hounds large like this?* The thought of Hazen being this big makes my core clench, though I'm sore from last night.

"Do you already want more?" Ledger's rough voice makes me jolt.

I look up to see him watching me and shake my head. "No. I—"

He chuckles. "I'm kidding, Asura." He rolls over, grabbing his phone and looking at the time with one eye open. "Ugh, Khazon is looking for me."

A chuckle leaves my lips, almost forgetting that we are forbad to see each other. "Are you going to get in trouble?"

He sits up, running a hand through his hair. "No. Today's my day off, and he's just wondering where I went after last night."

I stare at his back, seeing way more scars. Slowly, I crawl to him, kneeling behind him. "I thought hellhounds heal fast."

His head turns slightly to me. "Depends on what kind of wound. From a Soul Reaper's weapon? That will leave a scar."

"Did… Khazon do this to you?" I reach up and softly touch one.

He chuckles. "Some, but none of them were on purpose."

"Good. I don't want any more of a reason to kick his ass," I mutter, crawling out of bed and standing naked in front of him. I feel his eyes on me as I throw my hands over my head and stretch before moving to the bathroom.

"What's going on between you two?"

I scoff. "He hates me. Rightfully so, but still." After using the bathroom, I return to the bed, throwing my silver hair up in a ponytail.

"Why?" His crimson eyes follow me.

"You tell me how he's blackmailing you, and I'll tell you why I'm the wicked bitch of hell to him," I say.

He smiles at me, moving until his back is against the headboard. Sadly, he has boxers on now. I pull the blankets over my body, reclining against the headboard with him. "Khazon saved me from being expelled from the Academy. After my brother died, I, uh, went on a rampage and hurt people."

"I would do the same."

He cocks a brow. "I hurt my previous Soul Reaper." He touches the huge scar along his chest to his sternum. "That guy lost two hounds instead of one that day. He failed to protect my brother, so I failed to keep him safe from my wrath."

I look at the scar; it was his body's deepest and harshest one. I can almost imagine the Soul Reaper hurting him.

"Khazon is my last ever Soul Reaper, and if he decides I don't belong, I'll be gone." There's a frown on his face, and it almost makes me regret asking him what happened.

"Damn," I suck my teeth. "So, I can't brag that we fucked?"

He cocks his dark brow, making me chuckle.

"I'm kidding. Honestly, you and Khazon just work well."

He nods. "He's the best Soul Reaper I've had, and it might seem like he doesn't care, but he does. He's given Andrew time off when he needed it, Eames' money. He helped me grow from my brother's death and improve myself."

I smile. "Yeah. He has that effect."

He looks at me. "Now, your turn."

"Khaz and I have been best friends since birth. His dad, Death, was always around, and we were the closest in age. When I was eighteen, I left Hell and the Shadow World; I left without telling anyone."

"Eh, there's more, and you know it," he says, making my face heat up a bit.

*Asura? Blushing?* "I don't know. We've always had this bond where we just knew each other's thoughts, and we told each other everything."

"Except for the fact that he's in love with you."

I push him, laughing. "Oh, my devil! Stop it!"

He keeps laughing. "Why else do you think he told me to stay away from you?"

"Because I'm an evil bitch?"

He rolls on top of me, pulling me to lay with him. "That sounds accurate."

My legs spread as my core grows hot. I'm sore, but I think I can handle one more good beating.

He chuckles, muttering curse words in my neck. "Well, are you going to leave me now?"

"Only if you beg." Feeling powerful, I wrap my arms around his shoulders and my legs around his waist to pull him in.

The bedroom door swings open. "As—Oh! My god!" a voice comes.

Ledger and I jolt apart, and then I laugh when I see it's Killian covering his eyes.

"My friend, out of everyone!"

"You have friends?" I giggle.

Ledger hits my shoulder.

"Gross! You guys are gross!" he shouts, leaving the room and closing the door.

I burst out in laughter.

"I guess it's my time to go before your dad finds me here." He slides from the big bed.

I wave him off. "He's working, but you should go apologize to Killian for fucking his sister."

"Me?! You apologize! He's your brother." Ledger slides on his shirt and pants. "Do you think he'll tell Khazon?"

I snort, standing and grabbing my robe. "No. Killian knows what's going on, and he's not petty. Derrick, maybe, but he's at the academy today for training."

Ledger nods, fixing his dick, so it barely shows in his black pants, but I can still see it. "I should get going anyways. I have homework."

Nodding, I slid on fuzzy slippers. I feel Ledger's eyes on me, and I meet them with my own.

"How do you make everything hot?"

"I put on slippers! Do you have a foot fetish? Do you want more?" Chuckling, I slid to him, reaching up and pulling his lips to mine.

"Next time." He grunts, grabbing my thighs and pulling me up against him.

My legs wrap around his waist as I deepen the kiss.

"Fuck…" he grumbles, pulling back before we can continue. He sets me down, and he fixes himself. Whining, I walk him out, but Killian is nowhere to be found, so he just leaves.

On my way back to my room, I find Killian.

"That's my friend, Asura," he grumbles, leaning on the railing. *Okay, I'm an ass.*

I nod. "I'm sorry. It… just happened. I'll respect that if you want me to not do that again. I'm sorry, I didn't mean for you to see that."

He shakes his head. "Do you even *like* him, or was it just lust?"

I swallow. I haven't thought about that. I wanted Ledger, which was pure lust, but waking up to him and talking to him was… different. I missed texting him and being able to speak with him. He made me feel protected even if I didn't need protection. *Did that mean something more?* "I, uh…"

He looks up.

"I don't know. Probably lust. We can't date because of Khazon's blackmailing and stuff, so…"

"Is that why you have Hazen as a backup?"

My brows pull together. "Back up? He's not a backup; he's just…"

"More lust, Asura?"

I scoff. "No—no. He's uh… he's just a friend. I-I… What about Raven? We all know you like her?"

His face heats up. "No! The Son of the Devil? No!"

"Yeah. The kids of the devil don't like anyone… It's just…"

We stare at each other. I let out a sigh. "Don't say shit."

He burst into laughter. "Well, Dad always said you would need an army of men to handle you."

"Don't you dare say shit to Ledger. He'd never fucking shut up. Plus, we can't date with this stupid shit with Khazon and—"

"So, just seduce Khazon too and invite him into the harem. You both love each other," he says, walking away.

"Love? The Princess of Hell? No, thank you. Love isn't a thing for me."

He scoffs and closes his bedroom door.

I huff as I move back to my bedroom, just as my phone starts ringing.

*Ledger?*

Picking up my phone, I see "Haze" on the screen. I smile. Just as good. I answer it. "Hello, handsome."

"Good morning, princess. Are you in a good mood because you just got laid?"

I let out a snort, twirling my hair. "No. Pffft. What's up?"

"If you're free, you want to come to get lunch?"

I smile. "Yeah, that's fun. Give me twenty, and I can meet you somewhere." *What would I wear?*

"I'll send you the address. It's just a little diner, so dress for that."

*Reading my mind again.* "Okay, see you soon?"

"See you soon," he says, hanging up.

Showering quickly, I get dressed. I wear a black crop top with flames lining the bottom and black jeans with large holes in them with fishnets underneath. With sneakers on, I move down the stairs.

"Hey, Asura. Can we watch a movie now?" Fen says, making me twist around. *Oh no.* "Oh, are you going out?"

"Fen."

He shakes his head. "Have fun." I watch him move to the living room. *Okay, I did tell him we could hang out this weekend.*

I pull out my phone and quickly call Hazen. "Hello?"

"Haze," I start. "I promised my younger brother—"

"Killian?"

"No, Fenric. I promised that I would spend time with him. I'm sorry I forgot, and I can't—"

"Just bring him," he answers.

"Huh?!"

"I love kids. Bring him. It's just lunch, and I'll pay for him too."

"It's not the money, it's… Are you sure?"

"Mhm. Can't wait to meet him." He hangs up.

I can't help but smile. *Hazen likes kids?* I bite my lip, moving to the living room. "Want free food?"

Fen looks up. "No…"

"You're not hungry?! Fen! You're too tiny not to be hungry." I grab him and throw him over my shoulder. He squeals. "I'm kidnapping you."

"No! No! My shoes, Asura!"

I stop right before the door. "You need those, huh?"

He laughs as I set him down.

"Hurry up, a hound is waiting for us, and when he gets ravenous, he eats kids."

Fen chuckles. "No, they don't!" He slid on sneakers that were by the front door. He races to me as I open the door.

"Oh, yeah, what about the Little Red Riding Hood?" I say, wiggling my fingers and chasing him to the car.

# Asura

Hazen is waiting for us at the diner he invited us to, saving a spot in the booth. Once we get close, he stands, hugging me. Smelling his cologne, I smile right into his sternum. "Hazen, this is Fenric. Fenric, Hazen," I say when I finally come up for air.

When Hazen pulls back, he bends to shake Fen's hand. I thought the height difference between Hazen and me was ridiculous. "What's up, little man?"

"Hi," Fen says, a bit shy. He leans in and whispers, "Asura says you eat kids when you're hungry. You look like you do, so is that true?"

Hazen sends a smirk my way. "No...Only the bad ones."

Fen's gray eyes widen, but there's a smile on his face. "I'm good then. Asura is not..."

193

Hazen looks up and down my body, ensuring that Fen can't see his eyes as he does so.

I snort, pushing him into the booth. "Okay, sit down."

Fen sits inside as I take the outer side while Hazen sits across from us.

"How was your dinner last night?" Hazen's icy blue eyes lock with mine. I know he knows some of it, but he seems to know more.

"Good! Dad made the dessert," Fen answers.

Hazen smiles. "How good was it?"

I let Fen rumble about the dinner and how much fun he had meeting the hounds. After a few minutes, Hazen waves someone down.

When I twist to see the person, our eyes meet. His lime green eyes are rolling at me.

"Jiggie," I say with a smirk as he gets closer. He's dressed in all black again with chains everywhere and combat boots on. His black hair falls messily over his eyes.

He sends a glare. "Hazen, I thought it was just us." Then he looks at Fenric. "You have a kid?"

I cackle. "No! He's my brother. Fenric, meet Jigsaw." Fen reaches over and holds out his hand.

Surprisingly, Jigsaw takes it with his gloved hands and shakes his hand.

I hold out my hand for him to shake, but he ignores it. "I already know you. Where am I going to sit?"

I look at Hazen and see that he takes up most of the booth, so I tap Fen and say, "Go sit by Hazen."

Fen ducks under the table, climbing in between the wall and Hazen.

I scoot over and tap the seat next to me.

Jigsaw grumbles before squeezing in with me. Hazen flashes a grin as a lady comes over to take our order.

"The usual guys?" She looks at Hazen, and Hazen nods. Then she looks at Fen. "And what can I get you?"

Fen looks at me. "Cookies and Cream milkshake?"

"Make it two."

"And to eat?"

"Get them the same as us, please," Hazen says. "They will love it."

I narrow my eyes on him as she walks away. "Mhm. I'm trusting you."

Hazen looks down at his phone and texts someone just as Fen starts to talk about his day.

My phone buzzes in my pocket; I pull it out and look down.

**Hazen:** You smell like Ledger. Like… *smell* like him.

*I showered. How can I still smell like him? Jigsaw probably smells like it too. Fuck.*

The lady comes back and sets down our drinks. Hazen's usual is a soda, and, of course, Jigsaw's is black coffee. Fenric slurps his milkshake happily.

"Are you Asura's hounds?" Fen asks after a sip, looking between the boys.

"No," Jigsaw says.

"I am," Hazen says.

Jigsaw sighs and looks up. "You really said yes?"

"Yes."

I bump Jigsaw a bit, earning a glare. "You could also join this awesome team."

He rolls his eyes. "No, thanks."

"Why not?" Fen asks.

Jigsaw looks at me for help. Although I'm also curious, I don't want to push him. "Just not all hounds are meant to be with certain reapers. You have to pick hounds you trust and ones that trust you," I answer.

"Do you not trust Jigsaw?"

"Not as far as I can throw him. But if trust is there, sometimes personalities are off, and it won't mash. Jiggie is too uptight for me."

I hear him scoff.

But Fen nods. "So, you chose Hazen because he's nicer? Or because he's handsome."

Hazen snorts his drink, coughing.

"Watch it, kid."

We talk until the food comes. Jigsaw barely engages with us, and I can't help but wonder if I ruined his little date with Hazen. They seem close, though, because Hazen can get him to smile more easily than I can. I liked seeing Jigsaw smiling.

When he takes off his mask to eat and drink, I can't help but regret not making Fen sit here. I was curious to see his lips and smiles, but I never got the chance to because he put his mask back on as soon as we were done.

"Why do you wear that?" Fenric asks, looking up.

"Fen," I warn.

Jigsaw shrugs. "I'm a hellhound with a toxic power."

He nods. "Oh, you know, my dad has a toxic hound as well," Fenric says.

My brows pull. "Huh?"

"Well... he did. His name was Hendricks. Dad told me about him the other day and said he was one of his best hounds."

I remember Hendricks, but he died when I was younger. But... Dad always hugged and touched Hendricks, and so did I. Something isn't adding up here. I just nod and follow behind when we go outside. Hazen actually paid for us, and he bought us all waffles, but they weren't as good as the waffles that Khazon and I used to have, but I appreciate it. It was fun.

As we walk to a nearby park, Fen jumps around, talking to Hazen about something. It makes me smile and bump Jigsaw. "He normally doesn't have sugar, and I think he's jumping to be as tall as him."

He just nods.

I let him stay silent as I keep my eyes on Fen. After a few jumps, he grabs Hazen's hand, jumping around. That's when Hazen grabs him and throws him onto his shoulders.

"Asura! Asura! Look!"

My hands find refuge in my pocket before running after them. Jumping high, I try to high-five Fen, but he has to be up eight feet right now. He stays up there, talking down to us the whole time. He tells Hazen about his collection of superhero action figures and books. Hazen feeds into it, genuinely interested to the point that they fight about which superhero is the best.

I glance back to see Jigsaw watching us... me. His eyes meet mine, and they don't look away at all. I wink, making him roll his eyes, but I think he smiled.

At the park, Hazen sets Fen down, and he takes off. Thank God he's wearing a jacket because it's freezing, but I am not.

"Come on, Hazen!" Fen shouts as he jumps onto the seesaw.

Hazen's eyes widen, but he's smiling. He shrugs off his jacket and hands it over. "I have a sneaking suspicion that he likes me better."

"Ha-ha," I mock as he moves to go to the seesaw. Watching him try to sit on it makes me laugh, and He opts to push it with his feet as I pull on his jacket.

"Going to have a collection," Jigsaw mutters.

"Huh? Of jackets? Yeah. I'm going to get yours next, don't worry."

"Oh yeah," he teases me. "I was so worried."

I smirk. "I didn't want you to feel left out."

He snorts. "Oh, thanks. I would be honored for you to use my jacket once and never give it back."

"I'd give it back... in a few years."

"Oh, I hope I don't remember you in a few years," he says.

I know it's teasing, but a part of me thinks it's truthful about what he says. Jigsaw would rather not have anything to do with me. Like Hazen says, he keeps to himself and touches no one. I pushed it when I felt him in the diner, but I won't ever again, although he didn't seem uncomfortable. "So, uh, you and Hazen, huh? Secret lovers? Is that why you hate me?"

He tsks. "I don't hate you... But yeah, Hazen is my secret lover."

I chuckle with him. "He's such a bottom."

"Agreed... But, uh, I'm not gay, Asura," he says softly.

"Better tell that to Hazen before he gets his hopes up," I tease.

He smiles down at me, and I have to pry my eyes from him to look away.

"So, the mask and glove thing. Is that... because..."

"I burn everyone I touch. Yes."

I nod. "So, how's living with that?"

"It's annoying, but I guess I'm used to it."

Hell's Reaper

He's never felt a lot of things, huh? I know logically, he's toxic and will burn through my entire body, but the idea of even him spitting in my mouth turns me on.

*No. Don't get turned on.*

"Yeah. Uh, that sucks." I step away from him. "You'll... make a good hellhound to someone someday."

He looks down at me. He's not as tall as Ledger, but damn near close.

"So, you and Hazen? Best friends, huh?"

Jigsaw pries his eyes from me slowly. "We grew up in the same orphanage."

My eyes snap to Hazen. He's sliding down the slide after Fen... *well, trying to.* "I didn't know."

"Yeah. Hazen was the cool kid everyone loved; he took pity and helped me out a few times."

"Nothing is a pity to Hazen," I mention. "You weren't a charity case to him."

"Yeah?"

I shrug. "Yeah. Are you upset that he's my hound?"

His dark brows are pulling together. "He's not actually my lover, Asura."

"I'm saying it because sometimes hounds who grow up together or are close are better pairs. I know you don't want to be my hound, so... I just want you to be able to work with him. You guys already have a bond, and it'd be so much stronger than before."

"Then you can't be his Soul Reaper..."

I look down. "You know, sometimes I'm nice. It's up to Hazen too, but if he wants to pair with you, I'm okay with trying to find other guys. I mean, who doesn't want me?"

"Me."

I snort. "Sure. I see the way you looked at my ass."

"What? How—?" He cuts himself off. "You're sneaky. I wasn't looking at your ass."

"Whatever."

It's silence between us, but I don't mind. I'm still watching Fen and Hazen play together.

"He's a good kid but very bubbly and energized."

I smile, nodding. "He's always been like that; it's insane. We were inseparable even more than Killian and me. Then I left, and I'm just glad he doesn't hate me for it."

"I think he's incapable of hating anyone."

I sit on a swing. Surprisingly, Jigsaw follows. I almost forget he's the teasing, toxic hound that doesn't want anything to do with me. "You need to take notes."

"People suck, and I know that for a fact," he says, very matter of fact.

"That's true. Push me?"

He scoffs. "Push yourself."

"I can't." I pretend I can't touch the ground with my toes. "Push me, Jiggie."

"Swing your legs."

I suck my teeth. "I don't know how. Come on. Be a doll."

He lets out a huff, rounds me, and begins to push.

"Push me higher."

I hear him grumble, but he does what I say. "Call me Saw; everyone does, not Jiggie or Jigsaw."

"Eh, I'm not everyone."

"Yeah, you're a spoiled demon who happens to be the next ruler."

I twist a bit to look back at him. "Yeah, so watch what you say, and would it kill you to kneel before me?"

He grumbles. "I'd never kneel before you." He moves from behind me, making my eyes follow him back to the bench.

*Challenge accepted.*

# Asura

After about an hour, Jigsaw and Hazen walk us back to the car. I can tell Fen is tired because of how quiet he is now. Part of me wants to scoop him up and carry him, but he's not the ten-year-old I left years ago. Plus, I wouldn't want to embarrass him in front of his new friend, Hazen. Once we get to the car, I tell Fen to get inside. "Sorry," I tell Hazen.

"For what?"

A smile creeps across my lips. *He's so fucking sweet.* He seems like he genuinely didn't mind playing with Fen, although I ended up crashing and joining them. I unzip his jacket and begin slipping it off.

"Keep it. Heard you tell Saw that you were adding it to your collection," Hazen says.

A chuckle escapes me. "Thanks. Thanks for lunch; next time, I'll pay."

"We come here every Sunday; it's a tradition. You can come again next time. Fen too."

My eyes wander to Jigsaw, standing off to the side, watching me. *Today was for them.* "Maybe a different day, Haze." I hold open my arms and give him a hug before directing my hug to Jigsaw.

He glares.

"Maybe next time?" I ask with a short chuckle.

"No," he grumbles.

"Bye, guys. Thanks again," I say, moving to get in the driver's seat. They wave to Fenric before we leave. Once we get to the edge of the Shadow World, the car wraps through dimensions and enters Hell.

I pull up and park, seeing Dad's car. Fenric rushes out of the vehicle, and I follow him into the palace, but when we realize Dad's in his study, we leave him alone and watch a movie.

Fenric falls asleep in the first twenty minutes, snoring away.

I pull out my phone, texting Hazen.

**Me:** Completely wiped my brother's energy.

He looks at it quickly.

**Hazen:** Me? I need a nap, too!

I smile.

**Me:** He's non-stop talking about you. He likes you more than me now, thanks.

**Hazen:** I like him better than you now, too.

I snort, rolling my eyes.

**Me:** Aw, thanks, ass.

Someone walks into the living room, making me look up. Dad comes in the room; his hair disheveled a bit.

"Hey," I say.

He looks up from his papers. "Hey. I came to watch the movie with Fen, but I see what kind of day it is."

Nodding, I turn down the TV. "We went out to lunch with Hazen and Saw."

His brows raise. "Who is Saw?"

"A friend."

"Like…" He moves to the couch. "A Ledger type friend or just a friend like Khazon."

"Which is less bad?"

He smirks.

"Why are you encouraging me to date so many guys?"

"Because! You deserve to be happy too!"

My eyes roll. "No, you just like the gossip!"

"*That too.* My life is boring, kid, and I'm not getting any younger."

"Oh, yeah. A thousand-year-old devil who rules Hell and the Shadow World has a boring life."

He snorts. "Smartass."

"Hey, Fen said you were talking about Hendrickson recently."

He nods. "His death anniversary was a few days ago."

"He was a toxic hellhound? I remember hugging him and stuff, though."

"Yeah, and?"

"Why didn't he burn us? Why did he always have nice clothing on instead of leather?"

My father's dark eyes narrow. "What's the sudden interest?"

"Saw is a toxic hound but wears leather and can't touch anyone."

He nods. "His toxic magic is somewhat immune to us. He used to wear gloves and leather, but the same witch doctor who made your meds has a friend who makes magic-resistant clothing and sheets and creams that help with breakouts. Hen used to get cracks around his mouth when he used his toxic spit."

I nod. "So, if I were to do something drastic like touch Saw, he wouldn't harm me."

"Correct."

"I don't understand why he doesn't want to be my hound. I'm strong but working on getting stronger with Hazen."

"He didn't want to be my hound either. They fear that they will do more harm than good in the group."

I nod. *I wonder if Saw thinks that.*

"Is Saw handsome? Do you think he'd like my pie? You should invite him to the next dinner."

I roll my eyes. "Go away!"

He chuckles but doesn't leave. "I used to have a harem, once upon a time."

I gag, rolling my eyes.

"Seriously!"

"Okay, we get it. I understand. You have too many kids."

He chuckles.

"Tomorrow, Hazen and I start training. Hopefully, I'm able to show Inarian that I'm worth being his Soul Reaper."

My father's brows raise. "Oh, Inarian? Who is that?"

"Goodbye, Dad!"

Dad drops us off at the academy the next day, being all sappy toward Killian, Derrick, and me. I roll my eyes, stepping out of the car.

I see Ledger sitting with a few friends and Hazen. Ledger's blood-red eyes meet mine. I remember the good sex we had together, and I bit my lips.

"Hey, there's Ledger," I hear my father say behind me.

Ledger waves, making me snort.

"Your boyfriend waved back. Aw."

"Not my boyfriend, Dad." I roll my eyes.

Then Fenric climbs into the front seat. "Oh, there's Hazen!"

"Hazen?" My father questions. "The one that you don't stop talking about. Maybe I should go say hi."

"No," I snap, sending him a glare.

"That's okay because here he comes with Ledger."

I twist to see them. I didn't feel embarrassed, although I acted like it.

Both guys are tall and hot as fuck. Hazen is slightly shorter, but only by a few inches. Ledger's faded shaved sides lead up to his messy black hair. His jaw has a bandage on it and a bruise formed, but nothing serious. He is wearing black pants and the black school logo short sleeve shirt. *Why does he make it look so… sexy?*

Hazen is just as bad. His Mohawk-like hairstyle leaves the top and back very messy. Piercings layer his ears and nose. He's wearing the same as Ledger but with boots and a few chains. I want to fan myself.

"Hi, Hazen!" Fen belts as soon as they are close enough.

Hazen holds out his hand to give a high five. "What's up, little man?"

My father steps beside me, the same height as them. He did that on purpose; he used his magic to be taller. "Hello. Fenric and Asura seem to be obsessed with you."

Hazen smiles very charmingly and shakes my father's hand. "It's nice to meet you, sir."

"Ledger, nice to see you again." Then he shakes Ledger's hand.

"Same to you," Ledger says. It was almost odd to be so respectful as he was asking to see the thong, I was wearing just this morning.

"Hazen, I'd love to have you over for dinner one of these days."

Hazen's bright blue eyes widen. "In... Hell?"

He nods. "I think we are going to have dinner soon. I'll let Asura know when to invite you."

He nods. "Yeah, that'd be great."

My father smiles. "Got to get the little one to school. Nice to see you guys!"

We say our goodbyes as my father drives Fen to his school, leaving the three of us. I start at the academy, and they follow.

"Are you wearing your red thong?" Hazen asks, touching the back of my thighs.

I hit his hand away. "Ledger just tells you everything, huh?" I glare at Ledger, who is just smiling.

Hazen chuckles, stopping me, and he leans in. "I thought you wanted to be shared, princess. Don't change your mind now." He whispers it right into the shell of my ear, making me shudder. "Have a good day, princess." He walks away.

I look at Ledger, who says, "I'm going to enjoy this teasing."

*Teasing?*

I learned first period what that meant when Hazen made a group chat with Ledger and me, talking about how I smell when I'm turned on. From then on, they flirt non-stop with me, and I do it right back. The classes are flipped today, so I don't see Ledger until

209

lunch. We share small looks, but because of Khazon, we can't talk.

"How does it feel to live the dream every girl wants?" Amos says after I explain the weekend.

I snort. "Please, it's just fun, right? It won't last."

"Maybe. But at the very least, they like you."

"Want to see something? I've been saving this all day." I ask mischievously.

Amos nods. I pat the seat next to me, and she moves around the table.

I go to the group chat and send the beautiful ass picture that I took in the bathroom I can see the outline of my pussy from this position. A red string runs through the swells of my ass and connects to the lace around my waist. I set down my phone, and we watch Hazen and Ledger at the table.

Hazen is the first to open the message, gasping so hard he snorts his drink. It ends with him coughing so hard that I can hear it.

Amos laughed beside me.

The table is staring at Hazen, but he refuses to show anyone his phone.

*Good boy.*

While the focus is on Hazen, Ledger looks down at his phone. His jaw tightens as his eyes meet mine. They are filled with lust, a darker shade of red than they usually are.

I wink at him.

He licks his lips, smirking and shaking his head.

"Damn. I want a harem." Amos sighs.

Jigsaw enters the cafeteria just now, narrowing his eyes on Hazen, who hasn't recovered yet. Hazen waves him on.

Our eyes meet as he walks to his usual seat.

I run my eyes up and down his body, seeing his everyday jeans, boots, gloves, and mask. His hair is pulled half back today, making my stomach swirl; I want to pull on his hair.

Jigsaw rolls his eyes, passing me.

"Tell me if he looks," I say, pretending to be on my phone.

Amos looks for me. "No... No... he's looking back at you."

I know my focus should be on being the heir and getting my team together. My whole life, I have been all work, training to be a soul reaper and take the throne.

The day I left hell, I was free of all the stress and expectations I put on myself. Quickly, I learned I became burnt out mentally, unable to function through the struggles of Earth.

Dancing was the first time I felt okay and was able to think. It made me forget about everything, and for the moment when the music was on, I just existed.

*I wasn't the heir, and I wasn't a burnout.*
*I was Asura. I was someone.*

211

## Hell's Reaper

But now, I'm all play, no work. Hence my brain is always on pretty hellhounds, white-haired vampires, or soul reapers.

The stresses of life won't weigh on me anymore if I don't let them.

# Asura

The self-defense teacher, Mrs. Hill, leads us outside toward the training field on the side of the academy, right before the Soul Reaper's dorms.

As we got closer, I saw others on the field. Mrs. Hill said we would be training with other classes, even higher ranked. Khazon stands amongst them, seeing the shorts ride up his thick muscular thighs as he bends to stretch his body. My eyes drop to his round ass, then to his veiny hands that grab one ankle.

"Don't drool," Amos says, bumping me.

I blink, itching my hair as if I didn't just stare at him. When we were younger, I liked him, but it never got past the crush phase.

*My main focus was being the heir and claiming the throne.*

Hell's Reaper

Khazon straightens and stands, moving forward to… Miya, who is glaring at me.

If looks could kill, I'd be six feet under.

I wave with a smile running over my lips.

Miya's lips move when Khazon gets close to her, and he looks over his shoulder, glaring at me too.

*What did she tell him?*

"Let's do a few practice combats!" Mrs. Hill announces to everyone. "Pick partners!"

Prying my eyes from Khazon, I reach for Amos, but she's already looking for her hellhound. I don't blame her. I would want to train and practice with them as much as possible.

My eyes move to Ledger, but a heavy voice boom right behind us before I can say anything. "She's mine."

I barely lay eyes on Khazon before he pulls me away from Ledger. Desperately, I reach out for the fire hellhound, but all he does is shrug helplessly.

Khazon places me directly across from him, eyes glaring at me.

"Okay, one partner will be on defense, the other on offense. You may begin."

Hearing that triggers something inside of Khazon. He lunges for me, quickly hopping in the air and kicking out. His foot connects with my chest, sending my ass onto the ground and my lungs gasping for air.

"Get up, *princess…*" Khazon growls.

214

Rune Hunt

With a few deep breaths, I finally get to my feet, only for him to drop low and swipe his leg over mine. I hit the ground hard, and he stands over me.

"So weak."

*Show him weak.* Circe says. Rage fuels a fire in my chest, clouding my judgment. I launch to my feet and start my assault. Every punch, every kick, Khazon blocks like it's nothing.

With a change of pace, he grabs my ankle and pulls my body hard into his chest. My palms press into his chest as a gasp escapes my lips. My eyes look up at him.

"Why would you fuck my hound after I told you to stay away from him?" he asks.

My eyes widen a bit. The rage burning in his eyes isn't something I've ever seen on him before. Khazon has always been calm and levelheaded, but right now, he reminds me of a madman.

"You really need to learn your place." He grits through his teeth, pushing me backward.

My ass hits the ground, but I don't stay down for long. I jump up, sending a punch and kick combo his way. One of my punches lands against his chest, but it barely looks like it hurt him.

He grabs my fist and pulls me close. His knuckles connect with my cheekbone. My head swings back, and my body follows.

"Khazon!" Ledger snaps.

"You want to know why I am faster, smarter, and better than you?" Khazon says, hovering over my body. "Because I didn't leave; I stayed and became better than you will ever be."

I scatter to my feet, ignoring the throbbing pain in my cheek. "I left with a good reason."

"No! You left because you knew you would never be half the soul reaper I am or half the king as your father."

"Fuck you! You know nothing about me."

His jaw ticks as he glares at me again. "Is the only reason you are here to sleep with hellhounds?"

"You know nothing about me."

"Answer me."

Ledger tries to intervene, but Khazon shoots him a look.

I scoff. "I don't answer to a low-value brand Angel of Death. Do you think you'll ever amount to your father? Do you think this worthless training will ever prepare you to take over what your father does? You're pathetic!"

"Me? I would never leave because my duties became too much. You're pathetic! You are no one. Hell is endangered because you'll be the Queen. You'll just abandon everyone, and hell will fall under your—"

*Crack!*

A gasp runs through the air as I slap him. He could have blocked it, but he didn't. The gasp brings me back to reality, and I glance around, seeing a crowd has formed because of him. My jaw tightens, and before he can say another insult, I'm moving to the dorm.

"Asura," Ledger calls, following me. He tries to grab me and pull me back to him, but I don't let him.

He follows me to the front of the dorm, where I hear Hazen's voice behind me. "Are you okay?" Hazen asks.

I growl, moving into the dorm building. I half expected them not to follow me, but they did—all the way to my room and even inside of it.

Pacing, I slammed the dorm room after Hazen entered it. "Who the fuck does he think he is?"

"Who?" Hazen asks, out of the loop. He was probably just walking past and saw us.

"Khazon!" I snap, twisting to him.

He looks down at me, eyes filling with... concern. He caresses my cheek ever so softly that it gets me to stiffen. "Did he do this to you?"

I'm assuming there's a bruise on the cheek that Khazon punched. I'm not used to someone being so soft and gentle with me... like I'm fragile.

"I am not fragile." I slap away his hand. "I'm not weak."

He holds up his hands and begins shuddering. "N-No. You are—I never said—" Haze looks like he felt bad that he offended me, but he didn't actually offend me. Something in me switches with him being all flustered. I smirk, running my palm up his chest to the side of his neck. "Look how flustered I make him, Ledge."

"He's speechless… That's a first," Ledger mutters.

Smirking, I grip Hazen's shirt and guide him to sit on the chair. The whole time, our eyes never leave each other. I straddle him as I did at the party, putting my finger under his chin and lifting it to me. "I am not weak."

His Adam's apple bobs before he speaks, "You are not weak. Confusing, but not weak."

I lick my lips before leaning in and softly pressing our lips together. His lips shock me softly, but I don't pull back. I want more.

Hazen's breath hitches, and his hands run up my back. I deepen the kiss, flicking my tongue across his lips. He groans, letting me in, and I take my time, tasting and exploring his mouth.

Ledger's warmth dances across my shoulders and back as he glides a finger along my spine. "Asura, you just got beaten and—"

I pull away, take off my shirt, and pull him into a hot and heavy kiss. At first, he wants to pull away but instead kisses me back. My hands explore his body, searching for all the soft spots that turn him on.

Hazen's huge hand grabs my breasts, and I arch into his touch.

"She needs to be very wet before she can even think about taking us," Ledger teases, pulling back.

Yes. I want to forget how Khazon made me feel. All weak and less than him. Hazen makes me feel soft, even if I don't want to be. I need more of him.

Hazen understands Ledger, grabbing my hips and rolling his up against my core. The sensation makes me choke up a moan, and I feel his smile against my lips.

*Cocky fuck.* Together, he and I move against each other until my clit is raw and tingling, close to an orgasm. I reach between us, unbuckling his pants.

Hazen is quick to help, lifting himself so he can remove his pants. We moan into each other's mouth as soon as my wet pussy rubs against his shaft.

"Oh, fuck," I whine, grabbing one of his shoulders.

"You really like grinding on stuff, don't you, princess?" Ledger's breath hits my ear and neck.

*I did.* It was one of the things I liked to do when having sex.

Ledger's hot hand grabs my breast and plays with the nipple. "Look who the dog is now."

I whine, thighs shaking.

"You need to stop." Hazen pulls back, moaning.

My eyes open.

"I'm close," he admits.

My hips roll faster, and I feel how wet my pussy has gotten him through my thin shorts.

"Don't listen to him," Ledger encourages, grabbing my shorts and completely ripping them from my body.

Hell's Reaper

I don't even think about stopping for one second. My fingers fisted his hair, pulling his lips back to mine.

"Asu—Asura." He moans.

"Beg. Beg, so you don't come on yourself," I order as my thighs shake. My breath begins to heave, and the thought of Hazen begging brings me close to the edge.

"Please, don't make me come so quickly." He moans pathetically, and his head drops back.

"Don't stop. You want that? You know you want to make him and yourself come," Ledger growls in my ear.

I cry out a bit, digging my nails into Hazen's shoulder. This is so overwhelming, and my whole body is tingling. I'm dominating Hazen, while Ledger is dominating me.

My head drops back. "Fuck."

Hazen's hands grip my hips, moaning. "Don't stop."

I want to smile at how quickly he wanted me to stop and now is telling me not to. I grip his hair and guide his face back toward mine. "Come for me."

He growls, moving his hips so his cock slides between my folds faster. It's soaking wet, coating his whole shaft.

Ledger's fist wraps around my throat, and he tilts my head back to look up at him. "Come," he orders huskily.

My eyes roll back as I listen. My hips roll in short bursts as moans fly from my lips. Logic and humiliation are thrown out the window. My back arches, and I reach up and grip Ledger's wrist. My pussy explodes, rocking my whole body. I cry out, and then I hear Hazen follow suit.

My glossy eyes look at him, and I watch his lips curve into an "O" and his brows furrow as his cum flies between us.

*Fuck. That was hot.*

"Lick it up," Ledger orders, removing his shirt.

I look up at him, lips parting. I hate being told what to do, but it turns me on when he orders me around. I slowly stand from Hazen, who takes off his shirt. His cum and mine are all over his cock and stomach. I bit my bottom lip, sticking my tongue out. Slowly, I run it up his long and thick dick. A moan escapes my lips as I taste myself on him. The closer to the tip, I taste his salty cum. I crawl up his body more and start licking the cum from the indents of his abs.

Hazen curses and closes his eyes.

Ledger's hand runs over the curve of my ass, and then his hand is gone.

*Smack!*

His hot hand slaps across my ass.

I jolt, gasping.

Hazen locks eyes with me, and as his smile curls upward, another smack hits my ass and some of my pussy.

I swallow the moan it creates, closing my eyes.

221

Ledger's hands adjust my waist until I'm on all fours over Hazen. Before I can ask what's going on, Ledger's palm pushes my head into Hazen's chest. A gasp escapes my mouth as he says, "Hold her still."

Hazen reaches and grabs my hips to hold me in place. My head spins with the endless possibilities of what could happen.

Then I feel Ledger's tip before he slowly starts pushing into me. My pussy tightens slightly at the pain of his giant, thick cock entering me.

"Relax, baby."

I roll my eyes. *You try getting a massive cock shoved into your small hole and then have it pounded repeatedly.*

Ledger stops, and I know he's not fully inside, but my hips have so much pressure from feeling so full. It won't take me long to come.

"Good girl." Ledger's hand slaps down on my ass.

I gasp, wiggling my hips to break free.

He growls, obviously liking it.

So, I pull myself forward and then push back until I can't take more of him. He stays still, letting me do the work by bouncing my ass backward.

It's not enough. I need more.

"Fuck me, Ledge."

He chuckles, and I know what is coming. "Beg."

I bite my lip. That's the last thing I want to do, not in front of Hazen and not to a man.

Hazen's fingers fall and find my clit easily. His fingers swirl, creating a deep need. My thighs shake, and I'm almost glad his other hand still holds me up.

"Beg," Ledger says, thrusting his hips against my ass. "Come on, baby; you know you want it."

My legs continue to shake, and I hold back each cry. But with each swirl and each clench of my pussy, I can't help but give in. "Please. Okay. Please."

"Please, what?" He cracks his hand across my ass.

I cry out, moving my hips. "Please, I want it. I want to be fucked!"

Ledger gives in, grabbing my hips and fucking me harder than I've ever been.

My mouth clamps shut, and I reach up and grab Hazen's shoulder.

The hand that is on my hip moves to my cheek. "Look at you. Kind of pathetic how much you want it," he says sweetly.

I close my eyes.

Ledger spanks me. "Look at who you just came on."

My eyes open, and I look up.

Hazen smiles. "So submissive."

"No. I'm not sub—"

*Crack!*

"Shut up," Ledger says after he spanks me again.

Hazen's long finger wraps around my throat as his other fingers keep up with my clit. "I think she's close."

"Fuck, me too," Ledger says with a chuckle.

I begin pushing myself back, meeting each of his thrusts. *I am close.* "Fuck. I'm going to come."

Hazen tightens his grip around my throat, and all the blood rushes to my head. That sets me into a fit of moans. My nails dig into Hazen as my legs close on his hand.

My whole body explodes. My pussy juices rush down my legs as I throw my head back and cry. After a few unbelievable euphorias, I bury my head into Hazen's chest, letting my body hit cloud nine.

Ledger follows, moaning and slamming into me over and over until he finally comes with a groan.

It takes a second for any of us to speak or move. I'm not sure I would know what to say or even how to speak.

"Surprisingly," Hazen says, pushing my silver curls from my sweaty face, "I had fun."

Ledger chuckles, pulling from my pussy and tapping my ass. I hiss, knowing I probably have bruises there now. If I can take two hellhounds and one spanking me, I can handle anything… I'm sure that's not the saying.

Hazen's hands find my cheek, brushing the bruises that Khazon made. "You didn't have to fuck us to prove you aren't weak."

I scoff. "I just wanted to dominate you, Hazen. Don't get the wrong idea."

His thumb brushes my cheekbone a few more times until he pulls away.

# Asura

I jog to my SR 101—Soul Reaper 101—class with Mr. Rickman. I'm a little late because of a short and quick meeting I had with the dean and my father the next day for punching people. My father asked me for more information, but what was I supposed to say?

A kid I've adored my whole life said I'm nothing to him and I am weak. His words played in my head over and over again until I was unable to sleep last night.

So, I kept my mouth shut. It's over and done with.

Mr. Rickman looks up at me when I walk in, and I hand over the pass. "Take a seat," he orders, handing over a piece of paper the class was working on.

## Rune Hunt

The only chair available is next to Khazon. Miya isn't here. My eyes find Amos, and she mouths sorry as if she did anything wrong. I take the seat next to him.

Sitting next to him reminds me I am weaker than he will ever be, and it reminds me of what he did to show he was stronger.

"Asura. Listen," Khazon starts.

I send him a glare before turning my attention back to Mr. Rickman.

"We were talking about how sometimes the setting can change how you collect souls or take down enemies. One is that if you were stationed in Hell, you must watch out for Hell Storms." His eyes move to me. "Not many have been in Hell before. Care to explain a Hell Storm?"

I feel like, in a way, this is punishment. Standing, I turn to the class. "Every few months, the...magic and Soul Reapers of Hell get overwhelmed. Think of it as...a toothpaste tube with the lid on, and someone is stepping on it. It's bound to just explode; Hell does that. The storms vary from toxic clouds to fiery rain."

"How do you avoid it?" a purple demon asks.

I shrug. "My father set up things that record the air, and everyone in Hell knows about it when one is about to happen. I've experienced it maybe a million times..." I remember the first time I was a child in Hades' Garden with Ozzy. He knew the sirens, but we were too far from his house to make it. He and I spent

227

the night in a tree stump, with me bawling my eyes out. "You go inside, and you stay inside until the alarms tell you to come out," I explain when I return to reality.

"Why doesn't it happen in the Shadow World?" a girl asks.

I look at Rickman. I know the answer. I could teach them everything I knew about Hell, but I didn't feel like it anymore. While I sit, Rickman goes on to explain how Hell runs on souls more than the Shadow World. After class, I stand quickly to escape Khazon, but he grabs my wrist to pull me back.

"I'm sorry for what I said."

I pull from his grasp as the room begins to empty. "So that gives you the right to talk to me like you did? Your friend?"

"You left," he snaps in a low tone.

"I've been your best friend for eighteen years; if I could have stayed, I would have," I snap right back.

His dark brows pull together. "What do you mean? Were you forced?"

My eyes scan his face. His dark eyes are filled with concern. His dark hair is the longest it's ever been, but it's still short against his forehead in curls. I always told him to grow his hair, but he never had the courage.

Everything in my body wants to forgive him and tell him the truth about what's been going on. Why I'm genuinely here. No matter how I feel toward him now, it won't change the fact that if I tell him, he will think Hell falls because of my shitty reign. That's the last thing on my list.

"Don't act like you care now, Death," I mutter, grabbing my stuff and leaving the room.

Amos finds me out of nowhere in the hall, grabbing my arm. "What did he say?"

"Tried to say sorry."

She sighs. "I'm sorry. I know how close you two were."

I shrug.

She bumps me. "So... you left with Ledger and Hazen and never came back to class."

A smile spreads across my lips.

Amos bounces so hard her blonde hair follows. "No fucking way... You had both?"

"Is that a bad thing?"

"No!" She throws her head on my shoulder. "How did you get so lucky? I thought Ledger didn't want to share?"

At the mention of Ledger, I see him moving into the locker rooms to get change. As if he feels me staring, he looks back. He winks at me, lips curling into a smirk.

I roll my eyes, but I can't stop the smile forming on my lips.

"He likes you," Amos whispers as if he won't be able to hear that.

I bump her into the locker rooms. "Stop it." Apparently, you can slightly see the bruises on my ass that Ledger caused. Either the shorts aren't long enough, or my ass is too round for them.

*Oh well.*

Walking out to the gym, I see Inarian sitting alone, eyes glued on Ledger. Ledger stares right back. I don't understand their lover's quarrel. Do they hate each other because one is fire and the other ice, or do they secretly want to fuck each other?

The second one sounds nice.

I bump Ledger when I get close to him. I wait until he pries his eyes from Inarian. "Are you guys going to fuck?"

He glares are me.

"Stare at each other any longer, and you might end up fucking," I say with a shrug.

"She's not wrong." Amos agrees. "I can basically taste the sexual tension."

Ledger growls, but it rumbles straight to my pussy. The way he looks at me, I can tell he smells it too.

"Not my fault," I mutter as Mrs. Hill tells us to get to our partners. I watch Ledger's eyes as I move to Inarian. He's pissed, I can tell. But somewhere inside his delicious self, he's happy I'm horny over him.

"Watch it," Inarian's rough voice comes as his hands grab my shoulders to stop me from moving. "Once again, head in the fucking cloud of dicks."

I roll my eyes, looking up at him. "Good morning to you too, Inari."

"Don't call me that," he mutters, moving to our assigned mats.

"So, how should you kick my ass today?" I ask, stretching my body.

He stares at me. "Looks like someone already did."

I look up, seeing his dark eyes glued to my hip. I know he sees the bruises.

"Did death's son fuck you up?" He slowly pries his eyes from it.

My eyes drop to his crotch, and I see how hard he is. The sweats barely hide anything. "Looks like someone's a sadist."

His eyes narrow. "Fuck you, princess."

"You want to?"

Without another word, he attacks, fist flying toward my head. I can tell he's pulling his punches, but still, I dodge. I grab his wrist. "Just admit it, Inari." It seems like I tend to make men pissed off at me a lot but fighting Inarian will help me train and be stronger.

"Stop. Calling. Me. That." He throws combos, and I dodge each and every one.

"Let's make this interesting." I grab his wrist again, pulling his large body against mine. "I win this fight; you are my hellhound."

He pushes away from me. "No. I would never work under someone who just got her ass kicked."

I scoff. "You got hard from the bruises on my hip, and I could be getting beat for all you know."

"Wouldn't be surprised with that hot head over there." He jerks his chin to Ledger, who is sparring with Amos.

"He would never." I mean… he did, but I consented. If he ever put his hands on me, he would have to deal with my father and his demon sons, but even worse …me.

Inarian's brows bounce. "Are you sure about that? What about Desi?"

My lips close.

"You think if I were your hound, your boyfriend over there would be okay with it? With me touching you, me being controlled by you?"

"I wouldn't control any of you. We would be a team."

"A team that you're in charge of," he says. "I'd have to listen to every call you make, even if I don't agree."

Something's different right now…The ground rumbles ever so slightly, and the air thickens and tastes…sour. To others, no one else would notice something like this.

"You know what, let's make that bet. You take me down right now; I'll be your hound. But you'll never be able to take me down because you're just as weak as I think you are."

I stare at the ground, trying to tune into my body more.

"Are you ready?"

"No… Wait! Something's wrong."

"What?" Inarian asks.

I lick my lips, tasting the acidity in the air. I've tasted it too many times before. "What do you smell? What do you taste?"

His brows pull together, but he inhales. "Uh, smells like... Jigsaw when he sweats. Tastes like sour candy."

One, that Jigsaw comment was *yummy*. Two, I know this. I move to the window and see it in the distance.

"Asura?"

I twist around, moving to the teacher. "Can I go to the office?"

"Go ahead," she says, turning her attention to the other students.

I try to walk out normally, but Inarian is close behind. "What is going on?" He grabs my wrist when we make it out in the hall. "What are you doing?"

"What are *you* doing?" Ledger's voice comes. "Hands off of her."

Inarian rolls his eyes and lets me go. "What's going..." He must have felt what I was talking about because his eyes moved to the windows in the hall. "What...is that?"

Ledger looks outside. "Asura?"

Gray and lime-green clouds have formed over the front of the campus, and lightning strikes brighten it up. The rain hasn't started yet, and the air isn't unbearable.

"I think it's a Hell Storm," I confess.

Their eyes snap to me.

"The thing that has never happened in the Shadow World?" Amos asks. "The thing we just learned about today?"

"It sounds crazy." I run a hand through my hair. I'm not even sure what to do. I was thinking of going to the dean's office and hoping my father would still be there or if they would allow me to call him. My phone doesn't reach Hell. I shrug, turning the corner. Just as I'm about to, I bump into someone—a hand steadies me.

I look up to see the tall, almost scrawny Ozias standing there. I half expect him to say something smart-mouthed like he normally would.

Instead, he bites his bottom lip, black eyes looking down at me. "Uh, Hell Storm?"

I nod. "Yeah."

"Cool. I'm not crazy. Where are we going?"

"Office…? Can you call your dad and mine?"

He nods.

"Asura, I have to find…" Ledger starts.

Twisting, I look up at him. "Go get your reaper and warn him, he knows what to do, and you can help him."

He opens his mouth and then closes it. "Asura…"

I roll my eyes, reaching up and pulling his chin down to me. I place a kiss right on his lips, but it's brief. "Let's meet in the SR 101 class; it has no windows, okay?"

His crimson eyes scan my face. Right now, they look more blood orange and less red and angry. "I'm calling Hazen to come to you."

I nod. "Thank you." I almost feel bad that I didn't think about calling him. But my mind has been on warning everyone. Maybe Inarian is right.

*I'm not meant to be a reaper.*

My hand cups Ledger's cheek, and I can't help but be worried about him, but I do not doubt that he will be okay. He is capable of handling himself, and with Khazon, he will be even better. I watch him leave before I turn to the dean's office.

# Asura

"You're not listening to me," I state to Dean Moon.

"Because..." He starts with a sigh, rolling his eyes. "I have more important issues, Ms. Beelzebub."

I roll my eyes. "So, you're not even going to listen when I say that there's a Hell Storm about to start at any moment?"

"Where are we, Ms. Beelzebub?"

Blinking, I answer hesitantly, "In the academy."

"Yes. The Anima Messorms Academiae in the Shadow World. *Shadow World.* Not Hell."

My jaw tightens at how he talks to me like I'm stupid. I know it sounds so insane that no one can understand it, but he's not listening to Ozias or me. "Okay," I stand. "Come on, Oz."

## Rune Hunt

His dark eyes narrow on me, and his brows pull inward, but he stands and moves with me outside the hall. "What are we going to do?" He grabs my hand as we meet up with Inarian and Amos.

"Wait until it hits—" I say but stop when something shakes the entire school like an earthquake.

Ozias bumps into me, and I slam into the wall with a groan. I grab his hips to keep him from moving away from me. He grips the wall behind me, holding himself up against me.

The ground settles.

"How do we always end up like this?" Oz's deep voice comes.

I look up. Half of his hair is up in a bun. His eyes shine a dark purple now, and I know that to be his actual color, just like his mother's eyes. My eyes move down his face over the freckles on his tan skin, full pink lips, and jaw.

Ozias really did grow up. He's not the same dorky pale kid Khazon, and I used to make fun of.

"Because you always got me in trouble," I say, finally.

"Sure, kitten," he mutters with a slight smirk and stands straight.

"Asura!" Hazen shouts, and I hear his footsteps as he turns the corner.

I move from the corner and am embraced by the hound. His power shocks me as his lips crash into mine, briefly. When he pulls back, I glance at Ozias; he meets my eyes before looking away, jaw clenching.

237

"Wait, Ledger said you were hurt, and it was urgent," Hazen asks, looking me over.

"I'm not—"

We hear a loud crack of thunder, and the school shakes again, silencing all of us. The sound of screaming fills the air outside. Hazen sets me down, and we all rush to the doors; and just as I throw it open, people start swarming in front of the entrance. During a Hell storm, people should find coverage.

The rain slaps against my skin and instantly burns on contact, but I stick it out, holding open the door and pushing people inside.

The lobby becomes chaotic within minutes, and the dean and Mrs. Godlie, the nurse, are all out of their office, struggling to help kids.

Part of me wishes they would have listened. I know it's crazy and a coincidence I just "learned" about Hell Storms in class this morning. Everything is happening so fast like someone was fast-forwarding a movie. I've been here almost two weeks, and all of this happened so quickly. Something is going on, but I can't tell what.

My eyes land on Mr. Rickman, who looks up from the students he is helping. His lips seemingly curl into a small, knowing smile.

My brows pull together. *Am I seeing shit?*

A hand grabs me and shakes me back to reality. A girl begins talking to me, one I've never met. "Your brother and a few others are out there."

"Kill?"

238

She nods. "A few scared girls rushed to the shed, and he went after them on the training field."

I've seen that shed before, and I doubt it'll survive much more. But what can I do out there?

"Should we go out to get him?" Hazen asks.

I shake my head, eyes saddening. "We would get burnt in the acid rain. But we can't just leave."

"I'll go out and get them somewhere else," Jigsaw says, shrugging off his jacket. *Where the fuck did he come from? I shake my head, no time to ask.*

Because I know people are getting hurt very quickly, I move my eyes down his broad, muscular frame, taking in all the tattoos peeking out from his tank top. A leather harness sits over his chest and around his shoulders, making them look bigger.

He takes off his mask and drops it.

I look up at Jigsaw. There are small scars around his lips, but he doesn't seem to mind me seeing them.

"Jigsaw, I can't ask you to do this." I push him back from the door.

His lime-green eyes drop to my palm on his chest, but sadly, he still has a shirt on. "We both know I can take the acid storm."

"It's more than that! Stop trying to be a fucking hero."

His eyes glance behind me. Before another word can come from my mouth, a huge arm wraps around me, and Jigsaw rushes out the door.

"No!" My heart lunges, and electricity surrounds me. Hazen. My hellhound.

"He might be able to make it," Ozias says.

I rip myself from Hazen. "No! The Shadow World isn't made for the hell's storm. The ground is going to give way!"

His black eyes widen.

Then I see a white flash running through the ground.

"Jigsaw!" I scream. Without another thought, I'm pushing back from him and running after Jigsaw outside. I hear Ozias and Hazen screaming behind me.

The ground rumbles with each flash; I push myself to run faster, just as the white flash shines in front of Jigsaw. My fist wraps around his shirt, and I pull with all my might to pull him back as the earth in front of him cracks open.

*I land on the ground, and a lighter body rolls on top of me. My eyes are wide as I look up at Ozias; His head hangs over my face, and I can see the pain of the acid rain soaking his back.*

*He just saved me from stepping into the crack of the earth. The white flashes opened sinkholes that are the largest I've ever seen.*

Jigsaw steps back as I land in the mud behind him. Putting my weight into pulling him back has stopped him from stepping into the crack. "What are you doing out here?" He scoops me up and rushes us both under a tree.

"Saving you." I grab his bare shoulders, and somehow his magic hurts less than the toxic rain.

He rips my hands from his skin and towers over me to stop the rain from hitting my face. "Are you okay?"

A smirk runs on my face. "Do you even care?"

"No," he deadpans, eyes scanning over my body to ensure I'm not severely burned. His leather jacket protected my upper body, just not my lower. "Don't ever come after me again! You could have died!"

"Are we going to save my brother?!"

His jaw tightens. "Asura. You are hurt."

"I happen to like the feeling of my skin burning off," I say with a weary smile. It burned, but after spending my whole life in Hell, I got used to it even if it feels like a parasite eating my skin rapidly. "Let's do this."

He curses.

I look at the shed that looks like it might collapse at any moment. "The reaper's dorm isn't too far. Maybe we can make it."

Jigsaw nods. "You go to the dorms, and I'll get them."

"Nope," I say, throwing the jacket over my head and taking off to the shed. Jigsaw catches up quickly, and we sprint until we make it there.

Jigsaw opens the door and begins ordering people to take off. They all listen, sprinting with cries in the air. When Killian moves to run, I put the jacket over his head.

"Go."

He nods at me, eyes worried. I'm his big sister and will do anything for him, even take the acid rain against my back. Killian takes off, and we follow. I feel each burn against my back that the rain hits.

The group all gets into the door, and I see a flash behind me; I glance to see a lightning bolt coming our way. I shout at everyone to get further into the dorm, twisting to open the door for Jigsaw. They push further into the dorm building until I can't see them as I reach out for him. Lightning flashes right under his feet. He leaps through the air, grabbing my arm, and *boom!*

The ground rips open right where his feet are supposed to land.

Our hands wrap around each other, and I prepare myself, bracing my legs on the walls as he lands inside the cliff. I jerk forward but not as hard as I thought I would. He catches his fall on the ledge. Quickly, I use my strength to pull him up, and he helps with his free hand. Finally, he makes it over the ledge. My body collapses on the floor, pulling his on top of mine. Half of him collapses on top of me.

"Fuck." I groan, pushing on his bare shoulder. "You're fat."

He scoffs, supporting himself on his elbows. His wet black hair hangs down in our faces. Slowly, a smile runs across his lips, flashing his canine teeth. I return the smile, feeling my stomach flutter from his smile. He lets out a chuckle. "H-how are we alive?"

I shake my head, still breathing hard. "No idea…"

"Are you hurt?" he asks, making me look up. He looks over my body again.

"I'm okay. Thank you."

He gets up on his knees, running his ringed fingers through his hair. Before he can even say anything, something flies through the air and hits his shoulder. My eyes widen as blood begins to leak from the wound the throwing knife made.

He growls heavily, twisting.

I twist around, and at the end of the dorm hall, I see a person with a mask. They reel back and are about to throw another.

Jigsaw's arm wraps around my body, and he lunges out of the way toward the stairs. "Go!"

Stumbling up the stairs, I round it, heading up the next set. Another person with a dagger sits there, waiting for me. They swing, and I duck, tackling them to the next flat level on the stairs.

*Who are these people? What do they want?*

I reel back, punching them hard.

"Another flash!" Jigsaw shouts, struggling.

The one below me reached for the dagger scattered from us when I tackled them. I lift my leg, kicking it further down the hall.

Their fist punches my thigh.

"Asura!" Jigsaw shouts, and I almost wonder what he thinks I can do.

Then I hear the cracking of the Earth. I rush down the flight of steps just as he grabs onto the railing on my flight. The stairs that are below him are utterly open to a giant cliff.

"Watch out!" he orders.

I turn to see the masked person coming my way. I dodge their attacks, narrowly getting hit by the blade. Twisting, I kick them backward again.

"I'm slipping."

Fuck!

Turning, I see Jigsaw's wet hands giving out. I lunge for his hand, grabbing it through the bars of the railing when his hands gave out. My head slams into the bar, making me very dizzy. But I hold onto Jigsaw, feeling my fingers tingle with pain.

*I need help.*

*Me?* the voice in my head whispers.

*Yes.*

*Mhm, I'm not sure about this, Asura.*

"Asura!" Jigsaw shouts.

I glance over, see a flash of silver, then feel immense pain. A dagger is sticking straight through my thigh. I cry out. "Circe!" Black surrounds my eyes as I finally let the demon inside of me out to play. I feel her horns scraping and pushing through my skull, creating a headache. My back aches from her tail growing from my tailbone.

Rune Hunt

"Finally," Circe's voice erupts from my throat. I watch as she grabs Jigsaw's hands with only one of hers and pulls the dagger from her lilac thigh with the other. "I got you, baby. Don't worry."

*Okay, good. Please...* My consciousness is leaving now, unable to see everything around me. *Save them.*

*Show them who isn't weak.* Circe says in our head.

# Hell's Reaper

Want a signed copy or merch of any of my books? My Esty shop is now live!

*The Flame of Hell holds power to all the underworld.*

*It controls all the souls, demons, and all supernatural beings living in Hell and the Shadow World. I am next in line for the Flame and becoming the Queen. To prepare for my new role, my father has given me one task before I can take over: become a soul reaper and find my three hellhounds.*

*Completing the task is more challenging than expected when two of the three hellhounds I've chosen don't want anything to do with me. And with people after me*

## Rune Hunt

*and my throne, I find completing my father's orders nearly impossible.*

*Now, it's a race against the clock to finish my tasks at the Grim Reaper Academy and claim my throne and the Flame before it's too late.*

# Hell's Reaper

Made in the USA
Columbia, SC
04 January 2025

51150226R00150